SEX BLOOD

RICK WOOD

ABOUT THE AUTHOR

Rick Wood is a British writer born in Cheltenham.

His love for writing came at an early age, as did his battle with mental health. After defeating his demons, he grew up and became a stand-up comedian, then a drama and English teacher, before giving it all up to become a full-time author.

He now lives in Gloucestershire, where he divides his time between watching horror, reading horror, and writing horror.

ALSO BY RICK WOOD

Chronicles of the Infected
Zombie Attack
Zombie Defence
Zombie World

Non-Fiction
How to Write an Awesome Novel
Horror, Demons and Philosophy

You know, I'm automatically attracted to beautiful—I just start kissing them. It's like a magnet. Just kiss. I don't even wait. And when you're a star, they let you do it. You can do anything.

Grab 'em by the pussy. You can do anything.

- Donald Trump, Former President of the US, 2005

Just pat her on the bottom and send her away.

- Boris Johnson, Prime Minister of the UK, 2005

GENESIS

CHAPTER
ONE

Slop, slop, slop.

Welcome to James's shitty little life.

He has to go last. Like always.

Which means his penis has two other loads of semen to contend with.

Sloppa, sloppa, sloppa.

Yes, her perky little tits are pointing toward him like two perfectly formed pyramids. Yes, she is squealing like a poor imitation of a cheap porno movie. And yes, he is enjoying having this beauty riding on his below average sized dick.

He just wished, for once, his friends could let him go first.

Slosh slosh slosh.

Tyrone and Liam have long since finished cleaning themselves up, and are standing at the side of the room, partially dressed, trying not to snigger too hard at the sight of their friend trying to find some pleasure in a vaginal canal lined with their lubricant.

James closes his eyes. Tries to imagine being somewhere else. Thinks of that porno film he watched this morning. The one where the woman's tied up and tormented; where the guys spit on her face and she begs for more.

Oh, yeah, that's the stuff. Beg for more, bitch.

The woman atop James slows down. His closed eyes must be annoying her. He opens them and stares at her. She smiles sweetly, evidently happy again, and resumes her aggressive humping, which confuses him, as the others finished by fucking her from behind; yet he's the one she gets mad at for using his imagination to become more aroused. Doesn't she realise that it's hard to be aroused by a real-life woman nowadays, when the women in porn are so much better?

And who even is this woman, anyway?

She'd come home with Tyrone and Liam. James had been busy getting his PhD ready for submission—it's due in tomorrow and is nowhere near complete—but she was keen to have all three of them. He has no idea how they talked him into it, as fucking a woman while his mates watched is hardly his idea of a good time and he needs to get on with work, but they somehow did.

His thoughts are interrupted by an increase in the volume of her grunts. She speeds up even more, and the slops become even more ferocious, and he wonders why she was so keen to have all of them; she must be quite sore by now, and he can't imagine she'd get any pleasure out of him that she hadn't got out of the others.

Also, there's only one donut left in the kitchen, and he wants to eat it before Tyrone or Liam gets to it first, so he urges himself to finish; desperate to wipe his friend's cum off his penis then have a long, shameful shower before getting on with his work. Yet, the more he wills himself to finish, the less hard he becomes. In fact, he's fairly sure he's losing his erection, and soon she'll just be fucking a soft, little lump.

He considers stopping, but figures it would annoy her just as much as him closing his eyes. Then again, wouldn't him losing his erection annoy her? Maybe he should just picture his favourite porn again, but try doing it with his eyes open?

He sighs. Why must he have this self-conscious inner

narrative every time he has sex? He's never just 'in the moment'—he is always thinking about how bored the other person looks, or how long he should keep going until it's acceptable for him to finish, or about what his mother is cooking when he comes home in the summer.

Then he asks himself why he was thinking of his mother, which leads to another round of *what the fuck is wrong with me?*

Her screams become more frequent. An exaggerated *ugh* on each thrust. Is she almost finished? Does she not feel pathetic, faking yet another orgasm? Or is this part of her fetish—that she enjoys being used as a cum dumpster for three guys?

In fact, why on earth–

"Aargh!"

The sniggering from across the room ceases. Tyrone falls to his knees. He clutches his crotch with a fierce grip, moaning and groaning.

Liam puts his hand on Tyrone's back and asks, "Are you all right, mate?"

Tyrone tries to speak, but before he can release a single syllable, he lets out a sickening roar and clutches even harder on his dick.

"Dude, you're gonna pull it off, chill."

"I can't help it, I—*awmafuckinggawd!*"

He falls onto his back, rolling around on the floor, kicking, shaking his body, whimpering then screaming then sobbing then growling.

The woman on top of James—Jennifer, perhaps? Tilly? Lequisha? *Fuck me, what is her name?*—slows down a little, smirking at the distraction. She looks inquisitively at Tyrone, then turns back to James and rides him harder still, with extra gusto, evidently not perturbed.

James is, however, quite distracted, as Tyrone's actions are nothing short of fucked up.

Not only is he writhing around on the floor, he is now punching his crotch, over and over, screaming, "Make it stop! Make it stop! Please, *make it stop*!"

"Make what stop, dude?" Liam asks. "What is it?"

"Please!"

"Mate, I can't–"

Then Liam's body convulses too, and he screams, and he falls to his knees, and he grabs his dick. And, just as he does this, Tyrone shoves down his trousers and pants to reveal…

Fuck, how do you even describe it?

His dick expands—well, not so much the dick itself, but the lump that has slithered down his dick and settled in the bellend. It grows and grows, glowing orange beneath his skin, expanding the head of his dick like an inflating balloon.

Liam is also wriggling, kicking the wall, striking his crotch, sending his fist against his genitals with full force, acting just like Tyrone; shoving down his underwear and staring wide-eyed at his expanding penis.

JenniTillyLequishaWhateverTheFuckHerNameIs is not deterred. James tries pushing her off so he can help his friends, but she just shoves him down again, pinning him down with both hands and pressing the weight of her body upon him, forcing him against the sticky bed sheets, and how is she so strong?

He tries to move, but can't. Somehow, this petite, flat-chested woman is holding him to the bed. And it isn't so much that she has extra strength—it is that James is weak; that his strength is diminishing, like he's becoming suddenly ill.

Then he realises.

Tyrone had fucked her first.

Liam second.

And James was third.

Just as he deduces what may have caused his friend's ailments, Tyrone's penis stretches to the size of his head and explodes. A mixture of yellow puss, cum, blood, and unrecognisable sludge lands on the walls and on the woman's body, mixing with her hair. It does not distract her from her dramatic grunts—in fact, if anything, it seems to make her more aroused.

Then Liam's dick does the same. Detonating with fluids James does not want to identify. His body slumps against the wall beside Tyrone's, and a puddle of blood from each body expands until they merge into one.

Then the woman stops. Finally. She lifts her head up, brushes the hair off her face, and grins at James. She's beautiful, with the kind of innocent face guys like Tyrone love to ruin, and guys like James are desperate to nurture. She has freckles across her nose, small lips, and a harmonious symmetry to her features.

She shrugs. "Sorry," she says.

She stands, runs a finger down the blood across her chest, then licks it as she saunters across the room, her delicate buttocks swaying from side to side, multiple men's semen running down the inside of her thighs. She doesn't care about the filth between her legs—it's part of the penance for her reward. The way she walks around the room with such pride, it's as if she is relishing in his friends' pain. In fact, as she walks, she seems to be deliberately stepping in the fluids that mark the carpet.

She bends over Tyrone and Eric—whose eyes remain wide and stationary.

Holy shit, are they dead?

Then she turns back to James.

And she waits.

And then the pain arrives.

It starts in his balls, and spreads up his shaft, then grows to agony in his glans. He tries the same techniques as his friends—beating his dick, squeezing it, even pleading with it.

But nothing makes the pain stop.

And she just keeps grinning.

She knew this was going to happen.

She meant it to happen.

James tries to ask, *What the hell is wrong with you?*, but the agony becomes too much for him to be able to talk.

"Whoopsy," Pandora teases.

And, as his penis expands, and he just about forms the opening plosive of the word *bitch*, James's cock finishes decorating the room, and his dickless corpse flops over the side of the bed.

She lowers herself to her hands and knees and licks up all the juices and eats every bit of flesh, filling her mouth with foreskin and puss and blood and shit.

Once she is full, she stands, licks her lips, redresses, and struts out of the room with her hips swaying.

The bedroom, previously full of toxic masculinity and talk of "birds" and "hoes" and how "these bitches deserve it", is now devoid of life; nothing left inside but three dead, depraved, dickless guys who will never high-five over getting laid again.

CHAPTER
TWO

THE CHRISTIAN SOCIETY IS, WITHOUT A DOUBT, MY BEST accomplishment. Never mind my first-class honours in my undergraduate degree, or being accepted into a prestigious master's, or the otherwise endless list of academic achievements I have to my name—it is this. A society where like-minded individuals can get together and socialise.

Except, are they like-minded individuals?

Not that I'd admit it to Mother and Father—the most recognisable faces of the church back home—but I'm not sure whether or not I believe in Christianity. It isn't so much that I'm an atheist, or that I'm even agnostic; it's that I don't care. I think there are more important things to talk about. I enjoy it because, when the society gets together, I'm in a room of people even more awkward than I am.

For example, let's compare my morning at home with my evening with this group.

At 8:00 a.m. this morning, my housemate, Dave, came home, still wearing the same scruffy shirt and tattered jeans he'd left in the night before. He strolled into my room, where I was still sleeping, and shoved his fingers under my nose.

"What's going on?" I said as I woke up.

"Smell my fingers," he instructed me, wearing a cocky grin I'm all too familiar with.

"Why?"

"Just smell them."

I sniffed. His fingers stank like fish and cheese. "What is that?"

"That's first year pussy, dickhead!"

Dave then stood, raised his arms into the air, and declared that he was the "king of all that is vaginous," before running through the house, singing "ding dong my dick is great."

Meanwhile, this evening, I am sitting in the middle of a circle, and to my left is an absentminded first-year boy with a face covered in pimples. His name is Gary or Larry or something like that, and he is sitting there, picking his lip, his back hunched over, staring gormlessly at our guest speaker. And to my right is another boy, unusually small, wearing a t-shirt that says *I open my PDF files with Adobe Wan Kenobi.*

It is the only place where I could describe myself as 'cooler' than most. I'm the nerd in every room; the man who's twenty-six and still a virgin; the thin, gangly geek whose body is scraggly and untoned because I'm terrified to enter a gym and be among so many alpha males; but here I am confident, and I am suave. I am the leader. I am in charge.

What's more, everyone is engrossed in the guest speakers I've arranged—at least, that's how I interpret their vacant stares. The guest speakers are a couple in their fifties with oddly red cheeks who gesticulate wildly when they speak. The woman's voice is so enthusiastic and overbearing that I can't quite understand how her husband tolerates her, whilst her husband is so camp that it's hard not to wonder if he's hiding something. They are both hugely passionate about the abstinence they are preaching, though I imagine it can't be tough for them to be abstinent when they are both so irritating.

"Your sexual sin does not just affect you," the woman,

Linda, says—speaking as if she's reading a child's book to a three-year-old. "This sin hurts others, too. No sin has a greater effect on your mind than sexual sin."

"That's right, darling," the man, Dylan, responds, his voice like he's presenting a game show, the huge shoulder pads of his suit lifting to his ears as he raises his arms. "As Peter said in his gospel, chapter two, verse eleven—dear friends, I urge you, as foreigners and exiles, to abstain from sinful desires which wage war against your soul."

"That's spot on, dear, and it also says in Corinthians chapter five verses nineteen to twenty-one—following your sinful urges has clear consequences, such as hostility, quarrelling, jealousy, anger, envy, drunkenness—and even *sorcery*."

Dylan took in a gasp so huge it's a surprise there's oxygen left for anyone else. "That is correct, my darling. You must remember, your body is not your own; it is God's."

"That is very accurate, my dear—the Holy Spirit is in you right now."

The holy spirit is in me? I thought we weren't meant to let anything inside of us—isn't that the point?

I look around to see if anyone else is sniggering at the unintentional pun, but most people look like they are singing songs in their head. Their eyes are empty, and their bodies loose. Honestly, I'm used to the sight—they aren't the most attentive and self-aware individuals.

"So how many of you," Linda says, "are going to abstain from sex like us?"

Linda raises her hand. So does Dylan. And they look around their audience with smiles so wide I'm not sure how their mouths fit on their faces.

Everyone starts shifting. Looking around. Was there a question? Unsure what they are meant to do, people tentatively raise their hands.

I raise my hand too.

It is a lot easier to tell people I'm a twenty-six-year-old virgin because I'm practicing abstinence, than say it's because the only time a girl has so much as kissed me was on a dare.

Upon seeing a few half-raised hands, Dylan and Linda explode into claps, jumping up and down, like a cheerleader after their star basketball player scores.

There's a cheerleading society as well at this uni. Another thing we've taken from America, along with Hollywood movies and casual racism.

Not that Linda and Dylan would condone cheerleaders, of course. I'm making a huge assumption, but I imagine they'd find a way to interpret skirts and pom-poms as sinful. They seem like the kind of couple who'd have a bible quote ready for all occasions; like someone would sneeze, and they'd start lecturing that person on the sins of phlegm.

As they finish, and people look around, wondering what they are supposed to do with their lives now, Linda and Dylan shove pamphlets in people's faces until they take them. Somehow, I'm not entirely sure these people will have much trouble abstaining from sex.

As leader of the society, I stand, thank our guests, thank people for their attendance, and confirm that we will meet again in a week for our next meeting, then after that for our summer social. A few grumbles of confirmation follow, and people filter out.

All except Sandy.

Ah, Sandy.

Long blond hair. Innocent blouse above small shorts and perfect legs. Always smiling.

She runs up to me and gives me a huge hug, and I feel guilty about the erection I get in response. She hasn't a clue about the effect she has on men. Every hug is innocent, every gentle nudge is without flirtatious intentions, and every smile and flutter of her eyes is done without knowledge of the hope it gives a man that Sandy might just, somehow, possibly, be interested in them.

I've done my best to keep her away from Dave. Whenever he sees a girl as beautifully uncorrupted such as Sandy, he declares he wants to "ruin her." I'm not entirely sure what it means, but it sounds awful.

"Thank you, Eric!" she says. "And thank you for your advice yesterday. You're right, everyone struggles on assignments sometimes. I just need to focus."

"I'm glad I could help. Hey, do you…"

I'm about to ask her if she'd like to get a drink, but the words turn into jumbles, which turns into some sort of skat singing, which turns into a brief hum, and I try to fashion it out by looking around.

As if I'd have the guts to ask her out.

As if I'd have the guts to ask anyone out.

"Are you okay?" she asks. I'm not surprised; I must look quite odd, stood here making all these strange noises. I sound like a dishwasher.

"Yeah, I, er… Well… You see, it's…"

Screw it. Ask her out. Go on.

Just do it.

What have you got to lose?

Then, just as I think I may have the confidence (which I undoubtedly will not), she says those dreaded words that make every man's penis shrivel up and cry:

"Aw, Eric. You're such a good friend."

And she hugs me. Kisses me on the cheek with no idea that it's the closest I've ever come to sex.

"Eh, Sandy!" comes a gruff voice from the door. A man leans in, big and beefy, a huge neck, muscles bigger than my head. "You coming or what? I'm parked on double yellows, I ain't got all day."

Sandy waves at me and leaves. "See you later."

And I sigh.

And I pack up.

As I do, I see another woman looking at me. From a chair toward the back. I don't recognise her; she must be new. Long hair tied back in a ponytail, a polo shirt over a long skirt. She looks like the good Christian girls I grew up with, except… she looks out of place in those clothes; like she should wear a tiny skirt or dress instead.

She smiles, nods at me, and exits.

And I am left to pick up the half-empty plastic cups of orange juice and sweep up the biscuit crumbs, wondering who on earth that woman was.

CHAPTER
THREE

I HAVE AN ASSIGNMENT DUE IN JUST UNDER TWO MONTHS. WHICH means I intend to have it finished within the next three weeks, as I do with all my assignments. If I set my personal deadline a month before the actual deadline, I will be prepared for any unforeseen eventualities that may mean I'm unable to finish my assignment for my personal deadline.

Not that it's ever happened. I'm not sure what such an eventuality would look like.

A hurricane, maybe?

Then again, I'm not sure we've ever had a hurricane in the UK.

It could be in case the fences of the local zoo break or shut down Jurassic Park style, and there is a stampede of animals that charge through student housing and break my laptop, thus destroying the hard drive that contains my work, and also somehow destroying the backup copies of my work that I email myself every day.

Again, it would be highly unprecedented, and would probably give me grounds to file an extenuating circum-stances form, but at least I'm prepared.

Perhaps it's to prepare for an even more unlikely situation, one that I often close my eyes and fantasise about: that I meet a woman. That we fall desperately in love, and I wish to spend all my time with her so struggle to fit work in. Perhaps we go away on holiday—so long as it isn't so expensive that I exceed my weekly budget—and we have a lovely, romantic getaway.

The stampede of zoo animals is probably more likely.

I often find myself catering for such an eventuality, despite such a fantasy never even coming close to reality. For example, I have two pairs of really nice jeans, and I always ensure at least one of them is cleaned and washed, just in case. I bought a cookbook hoping I could learn how to cook dinner for a woman. I even bought the karma sutra, but it just intimidated me.

Still, I know it's just a fantasy. Seeing as I've reached my mid-twenties without losing my virginity, and have only ever kissed a girl once (it was awesome until she started laughing and returned to her game of truth or dare), I imagine I'm fairly safe.

I finish the first draft of my assignment by 9:00 a.m., which is when Dave bursts into my room.

"Eric, you fucking knob, what's up?"

To Dave, this is a friendly greeting.

"Were you having a wank over your assignment?" he asks, looking over my shoulder. "You know there's porn on the internet, right?"

Again, this is apparently normal conversation to Dave.

"I tell you what, though; I am fucking knackered. Was up all night pooning this blond bitch."

Yes, this is how Dave talks, and yes, I think it's awful. Funnily enough, Dave can actually be friendly and charming —but it's usually when he's after something.

"Sounds nice," I say.

He walks around my room with his hands down the front of his tracksuit bottoms. He looks at my calendar: *Farm*

Animals 2022. This month's animal is a pig, chilling out under the sun, with half of his body poking out of his sty.

"Mate, what the fuck is that?"

"It's a pig."

"Yes, but why? You know you can get calendars with birds on, don't you?"

He doesn't mean birds as in animals.

"What do you want?" I ask.

"Dunno. Bored. Want a game of FIFA?"

"Maybe in half an hour, I've got work to do."

"It's Saturday morning."

I say nothing. I don't really understand why this is relevant.

"Dave?" a woman's voice calls from down the hallway.

"Fuck, is she still here?" Dave storms out of the room, and I hear him shouting down the corridor, "Ain't you gone yet?"

I like Dave. Honestly, there have been moments when he's been nice. I think. I'm sure it happened once. But, most of the time, this is who he is.

It makes me think of my sister.

We were really close as kids. I'd pick her up from school, we'd play Lego, or we'd play tag, or we'd dress up and perform plays for our parents. Then she entered adolescence and suddenly started calling me *dork* and *nerd.* She replaced the cute little dungarees and princess t-shirts with short skirts and low-cut tops. She gets up an hour early to put make-up on for school and seems to have a different guy's name written on her hand every month.

In a year, she'll go to university, and she'll meet guys like Dave. She will get screwed over by a Dave. And she will be guarded forever because of it. And I hate the impact that people such as Dave will have on the way she sees men.

Dave finishes chucking the woman out, comes into my room without knocking, and turns my Xbox on. I try working for a little longer, but he coerces me into a game of FIFA.

As we play, he regales his night with the woman he's just kicked out of the house, and I wonder how someone like him can get all these women, whilst I am always 'the friend.'

I try asking Dave how he attracts these women and I don't, and he tells me it's because I'm "a dick with no balls."

I nod along, not entirely sure what that means.

SHE PROWLS

She prowls the night clubs.

She searches for the right man.

She chooses student night; a night where posters such as *2 for 1 drinks* and *free shot for every woman upon entry* fill the windows of establishments guarded by men in suits with ID badges around their arms.

She watches men stumble from one club to the other, searching for female prey. The men wear shirts and the women wear dresses and the men wear smart jeans and the women show off their legs. Man after man follow those legs, under the misguided belief that those legs belong to him.

The more revealing the woman dresses, the more entitled a man is to her.

It is a fucked-up logic never acknowledged but always enforced.

It's like a nature documentary on mating habits. *She* can almost hear the voice-over: "The male finds the female with the biggest cleavage, and he approaches her, hoping she will fall away from her pack. She is highly inebriated, which makes her easier for the male to target. After separating the female from her friends, he takes her to his den, where she will have no recollection of whether she gave consent. In the morning, the male will gloat to the other males in an attempt to become the alpha."

Every hopeful man is a scumbag seeking another hole to aim at. The easier it is to aim at it, the more succulent the hole appears. *She* hates every single one of them.

It gives *her* the reason to prowl.

To survey the clubs. To watch the drunks. To seek the right target.

She chooses a club down an alley. Dark, but popular. *She* shows her ID. They let *her* in before the queue of men, who verbally object to *her* skipping the queue as they rape *her* with their eyes.

The interior smells like smoke machines and cheap deodorant. The dance floor is sticky on her high heels. There are a several tables, but only a few have chairs. Many drinks are left unattended on the bar or on a stool. A clump of desperate men surrounds a group of scantily clad women who push themselves against the bar, their breasts helping them get served first.

She smiles at the stupidity. Everyone here is compensating for something. Whether low self-esteem or a desperate sexual appetite, it is a cesspool of insecurity.

A man passes a group of women and runs his hands against the buttocks of someone wearing a glittery pink dress. The woman turns around and confronts him. He claims it was unintentional. An impasse settles between them where he waits to see if she calls him on his bullshit. His mates snigger. He carries on walking. Later on in the night, *she* sees him pretend a woman's breasts are airhorns. The woman laughs it off, but in her eyes *she* sees the death of this woman's belief; the destruction of the notion that the kind of men portrayed in Disney movies do exist. In a few years, a cynical belief that all men are responsible for misogyny will become her perpetual narrative, and she will react with anger to any man who says *I'm not like that.*

She follows a pair of women to the dance floor. *She* knows those women; not personally, but *she's* seen them all before. The younger one looks forward to a night of dancing, whilst the older one is worried about a night of groping and unwanted advances and having her drink spiked. *She* isn't sure any of these women are having fun. *She* isn't sure any man is either. *She* predicts that the younger one will hook up with a guy, but will be too wasted to participate in sex, and when she wakes up with semen dripping from her cunt, the police will tell her that if she's too drunk to remember if she gave consent, then they don't have a case to prove. Trying to propose the logic that a drunk woman can't give consent will be about as useful as explaining everyday sexism to the man *she* sees dry humping a woman at the bar to make his friends snigger.

The lads laugh. The girl tuts. The lads forget it ever happened. The girl remembers it forever.

Her gaze drifts to a group of men surveying the dance floor. They are assessing the women. The criteria are: how little she wears, how sexily she dances, how many men she talks to, and how much she laughs. They use this data to deduce which woman is likely to be the easiest lay. If they put as much effort into assessing the morality of their lives, they'd probably solve world hunger.

Some women enter the dance floor with a male friend to put other men off. Other women dance in large groups so that, when a man tries to grind up against one of their friends, they can surround that friend and protect her. This annoys the men; the women gained entry to the club without having to queue, and this means those women are here for them. They lined up outside for ages to access these women, after all. The logic is pathetic.

She lets the night progress. The dance floor fills until it's impossible to throw any kind of move without touching another person. Men's unintentional groping increases. *She* tries to pick out the most prolific target. It's difficult, as they are all abhorrent.

Then *she* finds him.

His hair is short and sticky. His shirt is tight and crumpled. His jeans are baggy, and his shoes are grubby. What he lacks in tidiness, he makes up for in guts. His mates egg him on. To them, he is a hero. He can pull any woman he wants. Sometimes, he does it because he can. Because it makes him superior to other men. Because why the fuck not?

In truth, his ability to pull the opposite sex is not greater than his comrades; he simply has the audacity to harass a larger quantity of women, meaning the odds of finding one drunk enough to take advantage of are that much greater.

She enters the dance floor.

She pulls *her* low-cut dress further down. *Her* cleavage cuts off just above her nipples. *She* wears purple knickers, and you can just about see them when *she* lifts her leg onto a stool to tighten the buckles on *her* high heels.

Her thighs are fucking perfect.

She's asking for it, but so is he.

"Hey," *she* says, having to shout above the music. *She* moves *her* mouth to his ear so he can hear *her*. He's close enough to feel *her* warm breath against his cheek. *Her* lips 'unknowingly' stroke his earlobe. "I've lost my friends; will you dance with me?"

"Of course!"

His mates give him the thumbs up. *She* takes his hand and leads him to the centre of the floor. Other women glare at *her*. *She's* too attractive to be allowed there. *She* is not allowed to be one of them.

The lights flash and the music pumps and *she* turns *her* back to him and rubs *her* buttocks up and down his crotch. It's supposed to be a dance move, but they both know it's not.

When *she* asks him how far he lives from here, he tells *her* he's just over the road, in the halls of residence.

When *she* asks him if they can go back to his room, he can barely contain his excitement.

They leave the club and kiss against a lamppost. *She* shoves *her* mouth against his as widely as it will go, shoving *her* tongue over his like a snake searching for food. He tastes like beer and *her* breath smells like vodka and it's a perfect meld of drunkenness and stupidity.

They get back to his room. *She* lifts *her* dress off. He takes his clothes off. *She* kicks her dress underneath the bed so it won't get messy. They look at each other's naked bodies. His penis is small and his pubic hair is matted. *Her* vagina is shaved and dry.

She rubs her clit for him. Not in a way to give *her* pleasure, but in the way he'd have seen women touch themselves in porn.

He's not bothered for foreplay. He gives *her* lube, and that makes *her* wet enough, and *she* places him inside of *her*. He tries to go on top, but *she* doesn't let him. *She* presses down on his chest, grinding *her* waist back and forth. He doesn't wear a condom.

She feels very little. It's a mild discomfort, if that.

But *she's* not here for the orgasm.

She gives him one, though. It's part of the performance, isn't it? A man of toxic masculinity requires frequent maintenance of his ego; his mental health is at risk if no one caters for his arrogance.

It lasts three minutes and forty-two seconds.

When *she's* done, *she* doesn't lay next to him. *She* takes the chair from his desk and sits there. Then *she* watches him. And *she* waits.

"Why are you sat there?" he asks. "Why are you watching me?"

Semen dribbles onto the chair. *She'll* wipe herself off later.

She doesn't want to miss the show.

"There's space for two on this bed, you know."

She leans *her* chin on *her* fist and watches him like a professor observing a participant in a study. *She* wonders what degree he's studying. There is a book on sports journalism on the shelf. There is no crease in the spine to suggest it's ever been read.

"Fine, fuck off," he says. "Get your clothes and piss off if that's your attitude."

She can't help but grin. In fact, *she* giggles a little. It incenses him more.

"What the fuck are you laughing at?"

He stands, reaches for *her*, and *she* wonders what he intends to do.

She doesn't find out.

He falls to his knees.

She loves this bit.

He grabs his dick in both hands.

She doesn't know why, there's hardly much to grab.

He screams. His eyes widen. His dick expands.

She uncrosses her legs.

He punches his crotch. Tries to take away the pain. Begs it to stop. Asks what *she's* done to him. His bellend grows. It's glowing orange, pushing at his skin, stretching his frenulum until it rips.

She sits on the edge of the chair. Licks *her* lips. And in three… two… one…

Blood and puss and cum splatter over the walls.

She applauds.

He lies on the floor. Groggy. Blood pouring out of the gaping hole above his perforated scrotum.

She descends to *her* knees. Licks it off his legs. Holds *her* face next to the stream of blood until *her* skin is covered in thick, sticky red.

She fucks herself, and *she* does it how *she* likes it.

She climbs onto the desk and licks bits of foreskin off the wall. *She* fucks herself harder. *She* chews it. *She* swallows, and now *she* does cum for real.

She rubs her hands in the remaining puss, runs them down her body.

Once *she* is full, *she* uses his shower.

After a thorough wash, *she* takes her dress from beneath the bed and puts it back on. It's immaculate.

She checks the time.

It's only midnight.

She still has time for one more.

CHAPTER
FOUR

I SIT AT THE HEAD OF THE TABLE, AS IF THAT MEANS ANYTHING. It's the monthly meeting for the Christian society, where we decide on upcoming events and review past events. I enjoy sitting here, as it makes me feel like the powerful CEO of a major corporation—though I know that is far from the truth.

To my right, Adrian is talking. He is so animated that his arms almost assault the shy girl to his right, who retracts her five-foot frame in on herself. She holds a book to her chest—*The Lion, The Witch and The Wardrobe*—and ducks out of the way as he swings his exuberant arms around.

"And Jesus would have loved it! He would have loved it! He would have *loved* it!"

He's talking about the abstinence speech we had last week. Honestly, I only invited those people because we had a session to fill and they offered to do it for free. I think what they preached is nonsense, but these people apparently loved it. They probably share the same view I have—if I can convince myself I'm not having sex because I'm practicing abstinence, it almost doesn't hurt that no woman in the world will fornicate with me.

"They just spoke so much *sense*, and it was *brilliant,* just *brilliant!*"

He slams his fist on the table. My coffee spills onto the plastic surface. I wipe it up with the nearest bible and hope no one notices.

"Thank you, Adrian," I say, wondering whether I could get an early night so I can be extra early for my lecture tomorrow morning. "Anyone else have an opinion?"

Stacey raises her hand. She's a plump girl with orange acne spots (which is bizarre, who knew acne could be orange?), ginger hair parted in the middle, and an enthusiasm most would struggle to match.

"It was, like, so totes amazing. I was super in awe of the woman. She is, like, so my new role model—and the message they preached was, just, like, super awesome and amazing."

I nod. Stacey keeps talking.

It's not that I'm cynical. Honestly, I don't hate these people —I just feel like I've outgrown them. When I was a teenager, I went to Sunday School and Christian Summer Camp and Church Group because it was my parent's decision. Having had time to reflect, I'm not too sure Jesus cares about me. Or that God is watching. Or that He has a plan.

Why would God plan for me to be an obsessive, lonely, insecure virgin who doesn't fit in with other men?

Why would God give me a best friend and housemate who is exactly the kind of guy I resent?

And why would God care enough to intervene if He could?

"And I totally think we should help spread their super message. It was like, just, so totally amazeballs."

Amazeballs?

Holy cow, this is tedious.

Just as I'm considering taking Stacey's crucifix from around her neck and jabbing my wrists, the door opens and someone pokes their head in.

It's the woman I saw at the end of the last meeting. Blond hair in a ponytail. Dressed like a conservative Christian, with a polo shirt and cream trousers—she doesn't need to wear a short dress to make my libido go crazy.

"Sorry I'm late," she says, and her voice is forcefully delicate.

"Not at all, come on in," I say, and indicate the spare seat, trying not to stare.

"I was just saying," Stacey informs her, "that the married couple was totes awesome and totes amazing and I would just love for them to come back because they would just be so super awesome to talk to—wouldn't you say?"

The woman places her hands on her lap and smiles awkwardly. She nods, evidently unsure what she's supposed to say.

"Anyways, I so totally think we should, like, get someone similar again or something as it was, like, totes the kind of thing we need if that makes sense?"

"Yes, I think that makes sense."

I give a knowing smile, but no one picks up on it. Except the woman. And she smiles back, amused, then tucks her hair behind her ear.

"So, for next month, we have a talk by Pastor Jason Jennings called Technology and Faith." I lift a pamphlet up, and read the back. "It's time to face up to your online demons. Is technology stopping you connecting with Jesus? How do we find God in a world he wouldn't have wanted?" I roll my eyes. "Great."

Everyone else looks enthusiastic. Stacey does a little clap with her hands. Jackson gesticulates, and the girl next to him flinches.

But the woman across from me smiles, and it's different to everyone else's gawping expressions. It's as if she knows how I actually feel; the only person present who picks up on my increasingly jaded view of proceedings.

"I think that's all for now. Any other business?"

Stacey raises her hand like a five-year-old desperate to answer a question.

"Yes?"

"I am having a totally super awesome party on Saturday and it should be so totally super awesome, and you're all invited. It's a no alcohol vegan night, and I ask everyone to bring your favourite passage from the Old Testament to share."

Shoot me now.

"That's great, thanks," I say. "I will see you all next week."

Stacey bounces to her feet and enters an eager discussion with Jackson and the shy girl as they leave. I don't think the shy girl has ever spoken, and considering the overbearing dominance of Stacey and Jackson, her quiet nature makes her an ideal friend.

Everyone else stands, keeps their head down, and shuffles out. It's not that they are being rude, but that they seem to lack the social skills required to have a conversation.

Within a few seconds, I am alone.

Except, I'm not.

The beautiful woman with the ponytail walks toward me.

"Hi," she says, giving me a little wave.

"Hi," I reply, and my voice breaks.

"I just wanted to say… I really admire you. I think you're doing a great job of running the society."

"Thanks. That's, er, I… yeah, I try… well, you know…"

Christ's sake, Eric. This is why you're a virgin.

"My name's Pandora, by the way," she says, and holds out a hand. I shake it. It's firm. Her skin is smooth.

"I'm Eric."

"Have you been running this Christian society for long?"

"Just this year, I guess. I haven't seen you around—are you new?"

I hate how accusatory I sound. She doesn't seem to mind,

however, and smiles; a smile that makes my knees shake. Why do women torture me like this?

"No. Well, yes. I mean, I've just started."

"And you want to meet other Christians?"

She hesitates. "Can I be honest?"

I nod.

"I don't believe in God. I'm sorry, but I don't. The other societies are just full of such, I don't know… I tried the women's football, and they weren't really for beginners; I tried a cheerleading society, but it was so bitchy; I even tried the dance society, but the men were so… touchy."

I'm not surprised, with a woman like her. I imagine Dave meeting her, being charismatic and charming, then later telling me how he plans to 'ruin' her. Just the thought of it makes me resent him.

"Yeah, I hate blokes like that."

"Then I saw you…"

Her voice fades away. I'm not sure what she's said.

"You just…" She looks around the room, as if searching for the words. "I spotted you through the window the other week. You run this group so well, and seem so good at it, and you… I don't know, there's something about you."

"Me?" I gulp.

"Yes."

"Well, I–" I choke. Then I keep choking. She goes to help me, but I wave my hand, and she backs off. I let it pass. "Sorry."

"It's okay."

"I just—no one's ever… are you sure you mean me?"

She chuckles. "Yes. Is it okay, though, that I don't believe in God?"

I sigh. "Can I tell you a secret?"

She nods and leans in closer. She smells like lavender.

"I don't think I do, either. I've been having my doubts."

Her face lights up. "Really?"

"Uh huh. It's just all I've ever really known, I guess."

"Well, that's brilliant. We can be the first two non-Christians in the Christian society."

I laugh. "We certainly can."

She looks at the time. Her watch has a purple strap and an old-fashioned clock face. I like that it's not digital—not everything needs to be digital, and few people of my generation see that.

"Listen, I have to go to my lecture, but I'd love to see you again. Are you free tonight?"

I stare at her. "Me?"

I hate myself. Why did I just ask *me*? Is there anyone else here?

"Yes, you. Would you like a drink tonight?"

"Of course."

"The student union at seven?"

I think about that early night I was going to take. It can go to hell.

"Sounds good."

"I'll see you then."

She smiles that warm smile again and leaves.

As I watch her, I have a debate with myself: Is this a date?

Are we going on a date?

Or is she simply looking for a friend, and I'm reading something into it?

I don't want to be like Dave, seeing every woman as a target. And women are never interested in me anyway, so I decide to be realistic with myself: it's not a date. Why would a woman like her ask me on a date? She's just looking for a friend. They always are.

Still, I can't help but be excited.

I've never had a drink with a woman before.

CHAPTER
FIVE

I AM GANGLY AND AWKWARD AND I AM AWARE OF EVERY LIMB IN my body. My walk is silly and my voice is odd and my clothes don't fit me properly.

Get a grip, Eric.

It's a woman. Just a woman.

Except, it isn't, is it?

It's a woman who's willing to talk to me. Who's friendly. And kind. And awesome.

Although, do I know she's awesome yet? Am I creating an image of who she is before I've even had a conversation with her that lasts more than a few minutes?

Or am I overthinking?

Then again, am I ever not overthinking?

I sigh. Splash water on my face. Lick my lips. Avoid my reflection to avoid feeling even more insecure.

Why do I fall in love with any woman who so much as instigates a conversation with me?

I leave the toilets, fearing that she'll think I'm pooping if I stay too long. Then again, what's wrong with that? If I put a woman off because I poo, how am I meant to keep up that pretence for an entire relationship?

But there is no relationship. It's just a drink. And a conversation. In the student union. That's it.

"Sorry about that," I say as I retake my seat. I'm not sure why I'm apologising for using the toilet. "What were we saying?"

"You were telling me about your master's."

"Yes. I was."

"So why palaeontology?"

"I think it was Jurassic Park. I saw that when I was a kid, and I just loved dinosaurs. Is that weird?"

"Why would that be weird?"

I don't know why it would be weird. Why did I even ask that?

"I don't know."

"So, do you go digging up fossils or anything?"

"I have done. Lyme Regis is great for fossils—I went on holiday there when I was a kid, and spent most days searching for fossils."

"You must have been a cool kid."

It takes a moment to realise she's teasing me. She takes a sip of her vodka and orange juice through her straw, giving me a cheeky smile as she does.

"Sorry, I guess it's a bit geeky."

"There's nothing wrong with being a bit geeky."

"Really?"

"I think geeky is sexy."

"What?"

"I like a man with a passion."

Oh my God—maybe this is a date.

"Well, there are so many interesting things about fossils and dinosaurs and stuff." I feel myself get more animated. "Did you know over 700 species of dinosaurs have been discovered? See, people only know a handful, so they don't realise quite how many there are."

"Is that so?"

"And most people think that the T-Rex was the biggest, but it's actually believed to be the Argentinosaurus. That dinosaur's poop would be around twenty-six pints—fossilised poop is called coprolite, and scientists have studied it. That's how we know about the dinosaur's diet."

She raises her eyebrows, nods, and stays silent.

Am I talking about poop?

"So, er, what are you studying?" I ask, changing conversation.

She shrugs. "It's not that interesting."

"I'm sure it is."

"Not compared to dinosaur poop."

I laugh and look down. My diet lemonade sparkles at me.

"I'm sorry, I didn't mean to–"

"I don't mind."

"You don't have to say–"

"I'm being serious. I'd love to hear more about dinosaur poop."

I laugh. She laughs. We laugh together. A beautiful moment sits between us, where we have our first comfortable silence. We hold each other's eyes, and there is no awkwardness.

Then some arsehole breaks it.

"What the fuck are you doing with him?"

A bloke saunters up, a pitcher of beer in his thick fist that sloshes over its edge. I recognise him from the student union's meetings between the leaders of all societies—he's in charge of the rugby society. He always talks over me and refers to me as Dweeb.

"Mate, you are batting well above your weight, she is way too fit for you."

Pandora tries not to make eye contact. I can't help it. He's too loud. People are turning their heads.

"How about you come have a drink with me, and I'll show you what a real man can do, eh?"

I shake. I want to stand up to him. I want to tell him to get stuffed. But I know I won't.

I'm too afraid.

His shadow looms over our table.

"Bruv, this slut can come home with me, and you can fuck off, yeah?"

In a brisk movement, Pandora grabs my hand and pulls me away from the table. She takes me past the bar, through the door, and into the fresh evening air.

I go to apologise for the guy, but she shushes me before I can get the words out. We are walking away, and she hasn't let go of my hand, and I don't think I've ever held a woman's hand before, and it makes me feel nervous—but in an excited way, like the first day of university or giving a speech at graduation.

We cross the road, still saying nothing, and she stops beneath a lamppost.

And she turns to me.

Looks up at me.

Places a hand on my cheek, so delicate it makes my body shake.

She leans up, and she places her lips against mine. Softly, at first. Then harder. And she opens her mouth, and we are kissing. An actual kiss. One that no one has dared her to do. And I don't know what I'm doing, but I sink into it, and after a while I get into the rhythm.

When her tongue enters my mouth, it rubs against mine, and it is soft yet firm. I'm stiffer than I've ever been. My underwear is sticky with pre-cum. I rub my tongue back, then she retracts hers, and takes her lips away, but leaves her forehead resting against mine.

She sniffs. I'm not sure if she's crying. I don't think so.

"I'm sorry," she says.

"For what?"

"For that guy."

"Some guys are like that. It's not your fault."

She says nothing for a moment. Just stays close. Enjoying the touch of our skin. Her palm presses against my palm, and she interlocks her fingers between mine.

"I want to go back to yours," she says, her voice a strong whisper.

"Okay."

"But I don't want to have sex."

It's funny, the thought hadn't even crossed my mind. "That's fine."

"I just want you to hold me."

"I can do that."

And she kisses me again. Soft and firm. Fireworks and rockets.

Then we go home, and we stand in my bedroom, and I go to ask her how she wants to do this—whether she wants me to step outside while she changes into a pair of my pyjamas, or something. But I don't need to. She removes her jeans and places them on the floor, then takes her polo shirt off to reveal a vest. She stands, her perfect legs on display to only me, and leans her body into mine.

We get under the covers, and we kiss some more. It's a single bed, but it doesn't bother either of us—she seems to relish the closeness just as much as I do.

After a while, she takes her lips away, kisses my forehead, and turns around. She takes my arm and tucks it around her waist.

And this is how we stay.

It doesn't take long until she's breathing deeply. A gentle snore. I've never heard another person sleep before, and it feels special; the rest of the world disappears, and it's just us, here, in this moment.

I take a while to get to sleep, but not because I'm not trying—because I lie here, relishing the closeness of her body, not wanting to miss it.

It's the best night of my life.

And, when I awake the next morning, there is no way I could have predicted what was going to happen.

SHE WAKES

She wakes, and *she* knows what *she's* supposed to do.

He lies asleep next to *her*. Poor boy, *he* does not know who *she* is.

She watches him for the moment. *He* is what's known as an anomaly. An exception. And, even though most exceptions *she's* ever known turn out to have something hidden in their past—something that shows that they are just like all the other non-exceptions—this one is different. At least, *he* seems to be.

They all seem like they are different at first.

But *he* smells different.

The smell of impurity does not taint *him*. Impurity is a putrid smell, almost inviting in its disgust; *he* is clean, like flowers or air freshener, and *she* isn't sure which one *she* prefers.

She worries *she* might fall in love with *him*.

She must remind herself who *he* is, and why *she* is here.

She removes *his* arm from around *her*. *He* sleeps deeply, and *she* doesn't risk waking *him*. *She* smiles at *his* sweet face. Even in *his* sleep, with messy hair and drool on his chin, *he* looks charmingly dorky.

She steps out of the room. The faint repetition of the electronic music of Babestation comes from the television downstairs. *She* tiptoes down each step, listening to a woman tell her viewers to call the expensive hotline. *She* peers around the corner. The woman on television wears bright pink lipstick, pigtails, and shakes her naked rear-end up and down so her thin layer of flab ripples.

A young man sits on the sofa, engrossed by this woman.

"Enjoying yourself?"

The man quickly turns. He looks *her* up and down. He's already fucked *her* in his mind. He quickly changes the channel. He looks confused.

"Who are you?" he asks.

"I'm Eric's friend."

"Seriously? It's finally happened? Get in, Eric."

She steps into the room. *She* knows *she's* wearing nothing but pants and vest. *She* knows he watches *her*. *She* knows the effect *she* has, and *she* knows what he wants to do.

She sits on the sofa. He stares at *her* cunt. *She* leans back into the cushions, but doesn't cross *her* legs.

"I got to tell you," he says, "he is batting way above... I mean, fair play to him, but you are well out of his league."

"Is that so?"

"I thought he'd bring home some other bible bummer or something."

"How do you know I'm not a bible bummer?"

"Because you don't look like a frigid bitch."

He looks at *her* like *she* just asked the most preposterous question he's ever heard.

"I see. And what's your name?"

"Dave."

"And do you have a girlfriend, Dave?"

He snorts. *She* assumes it's an ironic laugh. He wipes a smidgen of snot onto his sleeve. "No."

"No?"

"Nah, I ain't the relationship type. I like all the birds."

"All the *birds*?"

"Yeah. I fuck 'em all. Skinny ones, fat ones, tall ones, little ones. I even fucked a midget once. Was weird."

"And do you want to fuck me?"

He raises his eyebrows and scoffs. "You kidding?"

She shrugs. "I don't kid."

"I mean, yeah, you're well fit."

"So if I was to offer to fuck you now, would you take it?"

He watches *her*. Considers. The answer is yes, but he gives *her* the same bullshit they all do.

"Nah, I couldn't. Not if you're Eric's bird. He's waited too long. And you already fucked him."

"We didn't have sex. We just cuddled."

He looks at *her* as if *she's* just said something ridiculous. "You kidding?"

She shakes her head.

"Fuck, Eric, what a pussy!"

"Does that change anything? Would you fuck me now?"

He considers it again. "Nah. Can't. Bros before hoes."

"So if I offered to take you upstairs and let you pound me until I scream, then let you cum over my face as I lick your balls… you'd say no?"

She notices his erection.

"Er… Course…"

She leans forward and enunciates every syllable. "So if I pleaded with you—no, *begged* you—to take me up there, do me from behind, then let me go on top, you wouldn't jump at the chance to see my tits and grab onto them as I cum."

He looks like he's trying to solve a hard puzzle.

"Er…"

"If I asked to tie you up, gag you, then tease you until you beg me to choke on your dick, are you saying you'd say no?"

"… What's your point?"

She stands. *She* removes her top. *Her* nipples are hard.

"My point is, I want you to fuck me, and I want you to do it now."

He finally looks like he's figured out the puzzle.

"I'll meet you in your bedroom."

She steps out of the room, then throws *her* knickers back inside. They land on his head.

He falls over as he chases *her* upstairs.

CHAPTER
SIX

WHEN I WAKE UP, THE BIRDS ARE SINGING AND THE SUN IS
shining and I am smiling and the world feels glorious.

But she is not there.

And the world is grim again.

I sit up. Look around. She's not in the room.

Her jeans remain on the floor.

Perhaps she's gone to the bathroom?

What's the decorum with this kind of thing? I've never
done it before; what do I do?

Often, in the movies, one of them goes out for coffee.
Maybe she's done that.

But would she have left without jeans?

I listen, hoping that I'll hear her pottering around downstairs or the toilet flushing.

"Pandora?" I call.

A door opens and shuts down the corridor. Footsteps
march toward my room.

It takes me a few seconds to realise it's Dave's door that
opened and shut.

She opens the door and her head peers around it.

"You're awake," she says.

I look back at her, confused. "Why were you in Dave's room?"

"Listen…" She takes a deep breath, goes to speak, then says nothing.

"Pandora, please tell me why you were in Dave's room."

I hear my voice getting angrier. It doesn't sound like my voice. I'm a pushover. I don't get cross. In fact, Pandora sleeping with Dave is the most likely thing to happen after I allowed her into the house, and it wouldn't surprise me; it would make sense. Dave is the one who gets the girls, and I am the one who spends my evenings living in a fantasy.

She looks back across the corridor, then steps inside my room and shuts the door. She's naked.

Why is she naked?

And there's blood on her arm.

Why is there blood on her arm?

At first, I'm distracted. She's hot. I can't help it. She's stunning, and she's naked, and she's standing in my room, and that should be a good thing—but I don't understand.

She steps toward me, crouches, and takes my hand.

"I need to show you something," she says.

"What?"

"It's… Look, it's something I kind of need to show you. It's not really something I can just say."

"I don't understand, Pandora. Why are you naked? And why were you in Dave's room?"

I rub my temples. It's too early for this. And I have a lecture soon.

"Please, I need you to trust me. I have to show you something, and it's going to be difficult to see, but you just have to stick with it, okay?"

"… Okay."

"Just—please—just trust me."

"Fine. What is it?"

She takes a deep breath, lets it go, then stands. She pulls

me up by the hand, and I follow her out of the room. Her dainty buttocks wiggle and it's so sexy but I want to be mad —and I am mad dammit!

She drags me across the hallway and into Dave's room. I've always hated Dave's room. The curtains are always closed, and it's always messy, and there's always a smell of leftover pizza, and there are always clothes on the floor.

Only, this time, amongst the mess and horrible aromas, Dave lies on the bed. Naked. His hands and feet bound to the corners of the bed, and a sock stuffed in his mouth.

"What's going on?"

I back up against the wall. Edge toward the door. She grabs my hand.

"Please stay," she says.

"Pandora, you have my housemate tied up and—"

"I asked you to trust me."

I hesitate. She did. But this is… This is weird.

Dave tries to call to me through the sock stuffed in his mouth. He's begging me to help. But he's also naked, and the woman I like is naked, and I don't really feel like helping him at the moment.

"Please, just stick with me," Pandora says. She places a hand on my face, leans in, and kisses me. Even her morning breath smells wonderful.

"Okay," I say.

She walks over to the bed. Takes another deep breath—she seems to take a lot of those—and places a hand on Dave's cock.

"What the–"

She puts her non-cock hand up to silence me, then leaves me to watch as she wanks Dave off. He looks to me with eyes of alarm, as if he doesn't quite understand why she's plea-suring him whilst tormenting him.

It doesn't take long until Dave has a boner. Once he does,

she stops wanking him off, gets onto the bed, and climbs on top of him.

She places him inside of her.

"Pandora, what the–"

"Please, Eric, I said to trust me."

"Trust you? I'm standing here, watching you have sex with—"

"Eric, please, just… have faith."

Have faith?

Have bloody faith?

She rides him, back and forth, gentle at first, and I am standing here, watching, as awkward as I've ever felt. I don't know where to aim my gaze. Do I look at his penis going in and out of her? At her erect tits poking at the ceiling? At her face as her eyes close and she leans back?

I don't know why I'm standing here.

I turn to go, but don't.

She told me to trust her.

I shake my head. How big of an idiot am I?

What guy stands by and watches the woman he likes shag his housemate?

She gets faster. I've only ever watched porn, I've never seen this live, and it's not as I expected it. He stares up at her, like he's in a mixture of pleasure and fear, and his breathing increases, and she moves quicker, and quicker, until he makes noises and he's shouting through the sock in his mouth and he's…

He's having an orgasm.

Inside of her.

Bloody brilliant. And I'm standing here watching.

When he's done, she dismounts and stands away from him. His semen drips onto the bed as his penis shrinks back to normal size—which is still bigger than mine.

I look at her, agape. "Why the hell did I just watch—"

"It's nearly done," she says. "I promise."

"Nearly done? I just watched–"

"Just wait."

She stands beside me and takes my hand. I let her. I don't know why I let her, but I do. And we stand here, watching Dave's naked body and his sticky dick.

I really do not know why I'm standing here.

I decide that this is ridiculous, and that I'm leaving, and I go to rip my hand from hers—then something happens.

Dave twitches.

His body convulses, and his crotch raises into the air.

His penis is throbbing. Up and down, slowly at first, then rigorous.

He screams through his sock, harder and harder, until muffled roars are all we can hear.

His penis expands and his bellend glows orange.

I feel her eyes turn to me. She wants to see my reaction. Like she's showing me her favourite film, and is worried I won't love it the same as she does.

But I can't look at her; I'm engrossed in what's happening to Dave. His dick grows until it's the size of his head. It is both intriguing and terrifying at the same time.

"I'd cover your face now, if I were you," she says, and she frees my hand so I can cover my head.

That is when Dave's dick explodes.

Pieces of foreskin and cartilage and blood vessels and spongy tissue fly around the room in a burst of blood fluid. The juices splash over every poster of scantily clad women, as well as every dirty, discarded plate; every unused textbook; every crumbling piece of plaster; every crusted piece of hand-kerchief; every box of tissues.

Dave's eyes are wide and empty, his body is limp, and there is a huge, bloody hole in his crotch where a dick used to be; a dick that caused so much anguish to so many women.

Pandora turns to me. She looks wary. Unsure. Tentative.

She takes my hand again, her body covered in remains, and she asks, gently, "What do you think?"

I look at Dave.

At the mess in the room.

At the gaping wound in the middle of Dave's body.

At the remains that drip down her torso and her legs and her hair and her feet.

And I say to her, with full confidence and absolute sincerity:

"That. Was. Awesome."

CHAPTER
SEVEN

WE SPEND ALL MORNING PLAYING.

I even forget that I have a lecture. Such things have become meaningless. I am embroiled in the epic yet tragic beauty of love; there is a greater plan for me now.

First, she undresses me, so we are both naked, then we stand and look at each other. I was so distracted by what was going on; I didn't have a chance to admire her body to its full extent; now, I inspect it; every crevice, every bump of cellulite, every perfect curve. Pimples appear on her skin as my finger runs across its surface, and her breathing quivers as she whispers that it is the most erotic touch she's ever received.

She gets to her knees. Runs her hands up my legs. Over my erection. Over my buttocks. Up my chest. Then she uses her tongue to explore my skin. I am scared about my body as she inspects it. I have no muscles and I'm gangly and my chest is flat and my dick is too small but, once she finishes and reaches my face, she kisses me and tells me it's the most wonderful thing she's ever had on her tongue.

Then we turn to the mess. The blood and the puss that decorates the walls and the carpet, and we lay in it and wave our arms and legs like you would when making snow angels.

We put our arms around each other and roll over, one over the other, covering our bodies in a misogynist's blood until it clings to our skin and drips off the tips of our fingers.

We kiss. Hard, until it hurts.

I don't enter her. I can't. We know what happens. She showed me.

But it's almost like it doesn't matter.

There is something so essentially primitive about the act of rolling in this bastard's blood. It feels like something our ancestors did, and something we neglect to do. Like something our species loses by labelling it obscene.

She licks the blood. Eats the bits of flesh.

I don't eat it, but I masturbate as she does.

Then she rubs the blood over her clit, then takes my hand and tells me to rub the blood off her. She guides my fingers, telling me what to do, showing me how hard or soft to go, and my fingers are wet and red and she cums—she actually cums—I actually make a woman cum.

It feels amazing.

Then we turn to Dave.

To the corpse.

She runs her finger around the open hole, accumulating pieces of gunk like she's running a finger through ice cream. She places her finger in her mouth, then runs the finger over the wound again and places it in my mouth. It tastes like rage.

Then she puts her hand into the hole. Waves it around, then takes it out, covered in blood and juices I can't even identify, and she rubs it down her face and her chest and her labia and her legs and her feet.

Then it's my turn.

I stick my fingers into the wound. Then my fist. Then my arm. It resists, at first, then I shove my arm harder inside, and ram it in until it reaches my elbow. I can feel more squidgy stuff and more juices and it's warm and squelchy and tantalising. She holds his head high, and we pretend he's a puppet. She opens and closes his mouth as I wave the body back and forth, his arms flopping about, and we make him say stupid things like "I abuse women" and "I will never fuck another drunk woman again" and "I deserve to be fucking killed."

When I pull my arm out, some of his large intestine comes out with it. I drape the end of it around me like a scarf to make her laugh. She smacks his dead face across the cheek with it to make me laugh. Then we wrap the intestines around the bedside lamp like tinsel and sigh as we revel in our pleasure.

We lay on the bed beside him, side by side, and our lips meet and we kiss and it's fiery and hard and passionate and our tongues dance about like a couple doing a waltz. We rub our hands in his blood, then spread those hands down each other's naked torsos, leaving red prints streaked down our skin. We lick the blood off one another, then flick our bloody tongue against the other's bloody tongue, and we laugh at how silly our frolicking makes us.

When lunch time arrives, we decide we're hungry, so I retrieve a drill from the toolbox under the kitchen sink, and I use it to penetrate his skull so we can cut off pieces of his brain and fry it in oil. We put it in sandwiches and eat it, our naked arses leaving blood prints on the sofa, and I add hollandaise sauce and the texture of the brain feels like firm fish.

We spend the afternoon watching pointless arguments between degenerates on the television, often missing big chunks of the debates as we get caught up in kissing. By the time the sun sets, the blood has crusted on our bodies, and it's time to clean ourselves off.

We have a shower together; the water soaking her body, outlining her curves, her skin glistening in the artificial bathroom light.

Once we've dried ourselves, and we've dressed, her

expression changes. She walks up to me, puts her arms around my neck, kisses me on the cheek, and says, "We need to talk."

"Okay."

She sits opposite me at the small dining table.

"We… we can't stay," she says.

"I know."

"I'm sorry to do this to you; your life is so promising, and I've ruined–"

"I'm not sorry."

She stares at me. She wasn't expecting that.

"Really?"

"No. Today has been the best day… I don't want it to end."

"It doesn't have to end."

"Then let's not let it."

She stretches her arm across the table and her fingers stroke mine. "They won't understand, you know."

"I know."

"They'll see that body, see what we've done, and they'll lock us away and keep us apart."

"I know."

"We're going to have to leave, and get far enough away that—"

"Pandora—I said I know."

She looks like she's about to cry. But she doesn't.

"I knew from the moment I met you that our lives were going to have to change," I tell her. "I'm ready for what comes next."

She nods.

"I'll put some clothes in a bag," I tell her.

"I have all I need in the back of my car. It's at the university."

"Dave doesn't normally show up to his lectures, so no one will be too suspicious, but his mother calls at the weekend, so we should probably leave now. Get a good head start on them."

"Yes. I agree."

I stand. She stands. We embrace, and we kiss.

"Thank you," she says.

I shake my head. "It is me who should thank you."

We walk to her car in silence, our hands joined and our fingers interlocked. When we get in the car, I choose the radio station that plays the best love songs, and we are on the motorway within minutes, leaving everything behind.

EXODUS

CHAPTER
EIGHT

AFTER THREE DAYS, THEY FIND THE BODY.

It takes another day until the women come forward.

At first, the headlines read *Student Found Dead* and *Murder at University* and *Young Man Shot to Death in Crotch*.

Then they read *Woman Comes Forward About Dead Man*.

Then *He Told Me I Was Pretty, Next Thing I Knew I Woke Up in His Bed*.

Then *He Spiked My Drink: The Exclusive Story About the Man Who Had His Penis Blown Off*.

I was tempted to keep that last one for a scrapbook—but, ultimately, this is not good: for three reasons.

First, we are suspects. They released mugshots of us from CCTV at the student union bar, stating that we are the last people to see Dave alive, and that they wish to speak to us.

We've had to change our appearance. This wasn't so bad for Pandora—she just trims her hair to her shoulders and dyes it red. But she made me shave mine. I've never shaved it before, and it looks weird. She tells me it looks cute, and that she enjoys running her hand over it, feeling it prick, but it takes some getting used to for me.

Second, Dave is not her first victim. I find this out in the news. There were a few blokes at another uni who died following a threesome, and a guy who was last seen at a local nightclub. Their bodies have also been found with their dicks blown away.

She didn't tell me there were others.

Third, all these women who are telling their stories about Dave—it shows motive. It gives the cops a reason for the crimes. Which does not help us going forward—it tells the police exactly how we will choose our next targets.

I feel like we have a purpose here. Never mind that dinosaur nonsense I was studying at university—we have a chance to do something *real*. Something that matters; something that will make a difference.

Albeit, it means the woman I love has to keep fucking the kind of men that I despise, and I hate that part, but it's important. We are showing women that these men have a reason to be afraid—and we are showing the men who don't fit in with toxic masculinity, and who don't strut around trying to take advantage of drunk women, and who don't contribute to feelings of insecurity women have when they walk home alone, that they can finally speak out. We are trying to change things for the better.

"What you thinking about?"

I look up from the bed. She stands in front of the cream walls of the hotel room, and I notice a yellow stain behind her.

"This." I lift the newspaper I'm reading and show her a two-page spread by a woman called Miranda. She's telling her story about Dave. Apparently, he said he would take her home when she was drunk and make sure she got into bed safely. The next day, she woke up naked and with semen on the sheets.

"Another one?" Pandora asks, snuggling up beside me.

"Yep."

"Do you believe her?"

"Of course, why wouldn't I? Isn't that the point?"

"I'm inclined to believe a woman every time, but not when they are being paid twenty-thousand pounds for their story."

"Is it that much? Wow, maybe I ought to sell my story too…"

She giggles, hits the newspaper out of my hands, and climbs on top of me. Her fingers interlock with mine, and she pushes my arms onto the pillow behind my head and leans over me. Her lips press against mine, and I could kiss this woman all day.

Then the kiss gets passionate. And she runs her hands down my body. And I run my hands down her breasts, then down her waist, and down to her buttocks, and then…

Then we stop.

Because we have to.

And she slumps onto the bed next to me. Sighs. We share the frustration in silence. There's nothing that needs to be said —the situation annoys both of us.

"What do you want to do tonight?" she asks, knowing what I want to do, but knowing that I can't.

"I dunno."

"Movie? Thinking we should lie low with all the news coverage."

I look at her. Smile. Think naughty thoughts.

"Why would we lie low now?" I ask.

She looks at me playfully; a devious look that I'm sure matches mine.

"What do you have in mind?"

I stick out my bottom lip and shrug my shoulders. "It's Friday night. Night clubs are full. Testosterone is running high. Women are getting drunk and men are groping them on the dance floor. I think we have a duty, don't you?"

"Really? Already? You don't want to wait longer?"

"I mean, I'm not pushing you into it if you want to wait."

"No, I'm raring to go. I just know it's… it's hard for you. Not being able to… Whilst I have to… In order to…"

"Can we stop speaking in code?"

She sighs. Looks down and nods. "Yeah, I guess."

"I know what I signed up for," I tell her. "And I know how much I love you."

Her head lifts. "You love me?"

"Would I do this with someone I didn't love?"

She kisses me hard.

"Go put on your best dress," I tell her. "Tonight, I get to pick the target."

"Whatever you say," she says, kissing me again. She opens the suitcase and sifts through her dresses and her makeup. I watch, amazed by it all. I've never watched a woman get ready before. I know it would bore most guys. I remember Father waiting at the bottom of the stairs for Mother on more than one occasion, tapping his foot, wondering why, if they were leaving at five, she was still not ready at ten past five.

But I find it fascinating.

This transformation she goes through.

Don't mistake me, I love her far more when she is in her pyjamas, but I can't help admiring how good she is at creating the image of beauty. She becomes youthful and energetic as the material items adorn her. The lipstick and the foundation and the dress are all inconsequential—it's the way she turns into the goddess all men crave.

After an hour, she is standing by the door, asking me how she looks.

I cannot wait for this evening.

SHE WALKS

She walks the night with *him* in tow.

Together, they mark the town with their revenge.

He doesn't know what's happened in *her* life; what makes *her* do this. The evident fallacy of the predatory male is enough for *him*, and *he* didn't think to ask if *she* has a bigger reason.

He did not enquire how *she* came by this ability, how this infection took hold of *her*, or how it manifested.

He did not interrogate *her* on the whys; why *she* hunts these men, why *she* is compelled to sacrifice *her* body to them for however long it takes to bring upon their untimely death, or why *she* decided it was *her* mission to spread this STI to those who it affects so much.

Nor does *he* know why *she's* with *him*. *He* does not know why *she* chose *him*.

He does not need to know.

He simply understands.

He has spent enough time being ridiculed for being unmanly. *He* has had friends who ask if *he* is gay because *he* doesn't want to 'mack on some hoes'—whatever that means. For so many years, *he's* believed that women are only attracted to toxic bastards. That they are aroused by men that beat them. That they crave the raw masculinity of someone who will mistreat them.

But *she* has shown *him* that is not true.

She holds *his* hand when they are out during the day. *She* is not ashamed to be seen with a man like *him*. *She* leaves *him* during the night, but only because this is necessary.

No one can know *she* is *his*.

Not until it is over.

At least, not until tonight's demonstration is over.

It will never be over.

This infection is not a curse; it is a duty.

It is not a burden; it is a weapon.

It does not need a cure; it needs a target.

She glances at *him* across the street, nodding subtly as *she* enters the club, and *he* enters behind, looking awkwardly handsome in a neat, red shirt. *She* wishes, for a moment, that this duty did not fall to *her*. That *she* could give *herself* to *him* fully, even just for one night.

But *she* knows what will happen if *she* gives in.

She knows what *she* will do to *him*.

Lights flash around the club. Music that's already too modern for *her* thuds through expensive speakers. Men and women barely old enough to drink gyrate on the dance floor, ignoring all their inhibitions.

And *she* tries not to think of *him*.

She's never had a *him* worth thinking about before. It's strange.

But *she* has to stay strong.

She reminds herself *she* doesn't even enjoy sex. That *she's* never enjoyed it. Such an enjoyment was taken from *her* before *she* was old enough to know that sex could be something one enjoys.

Every time *she* feels a man inside of *her*, *she* remembers what it was like. The dryness of *her* undeveloped labia. The scraping of *her* vaginal walls as something thick brushes against *her* cervix. The way *she* learnt that forced penetration was the same as love.

Even so, *she'd* love to give *him* the love *he* craves.

Even with what happens next.

Three men 'mistakenly' stroke *her* buttocks as they walk past, and another two insist on buying *her* a drink *she* keeps turning down. *She* looks at *him* across the club. Scanning the room for *her*. *She* meets *his* eyes, and *he* keeps scanning.

He's not looking for *her*.

He's looking for the target.

She dances. Sometimes with a guy, sometimes not. Often, *she* doesn't have a choice; a guy will choose to dance with *her* and *she* doesn't have any friends to push him away. A man can't hear her say no above the music, and it wouldn't make much difference, anyway. *She* feels them rubbing up against *her*, and it makes *her* feel sick, and it proves that what *she* does is right.

Then *he* makes *his* choice.

A man with his collar up. Three buttons undone on his shirt. Blue hair. What kind of guy has blue hair?

The target has been a pest all night. Women gravitate away from him, desperate not to be harassed. *She* directs herself toward him, rubs *her* hand across the stubble of a beard he's unable to grow, and dances down his body. *She* lifts *her* hand in the air, swaying *her* hips as *she* dances to *her* knees, *her* face brushing the target's crotch, and *she* catches *his* eyes as *she* comes back up.

He hates this. *He* loves this.

Who can tell?

She tells the target that *she* wants to go home. *She's* too drunk. Can he help her?

The target says yes.

She says *she* needs to get *her* coat.

The target says not to worry about *her* coat.

She puts an arm around the target to keep *herself* steady. *She* hasn't drunk anything, but as far as the target is concerned, *she's* drunk everything.

The bouncers say nothing. Women walk home in groups to keep themselves safe. The taxi drivers who wait at the taxi rank say nothing. *He* follows behind, but *he* keeps his distance.

She makes sure that, when *she* enters the guy's flat, *she* reaches behind *her* back and twists the lock until the door is open, thus allowing *him* to enter when *he's* ready.

The target drapes *her* on the bed like a dirty coat. *Her* head rolls to the side. *She* coughs. The target lifts *her* chin so *she's* forced to look at him.

"You're going to fuck me," the target says.

"I certainly am," *she* replies.

The target lifts *her* dress, slips off *her* knickers, and enters *her*.

He waits in the hallway. Watching. Waiting for the moment.

It takes the target two minutes to cum.

Then *he* steps into the room, and the pleasure can begin.

CHAPTER
NINE

WE LAY ON THE BILE LIKE IT'S A BED SHEET. OUR BODIES ARE covered, and barely a flicker of skin is visible. We are out of breath, panting from our excursions.

"Bloody hell," I exclaim. "That was even better than the first time."

She rolls over, squishing against part of the dead bloke's liver, and drapes an arm around me. We stuffed our clothes behind the television earlier, so that they remain unaffected by any wayward bodily juices—but neither of us wishes to put them back on yet.

She closes her eyes, and it doesn't take long until she's breathing deeply. Her eyelids flutter as she sleeps. I'm not surprised she's tired. Our frolicking takes a lot of energy.

Personally, however, I cannot sleep. I'm still too pumped. The adrenaline hasn't left my body yet. What's more, the blood is drying on my chest and my legs and it's becoming sticky. And my throat is dry.

And I can't fight a niggling feeling that… I don't know… Jealousy, perhaps…

I know I shouldn't. What she shares with me is greater

than sex. I think. I don't know, I've never had it. Perhaps that's what's bothering me.

All these pricks get to fuck the woman I love before they die. I don't even know what it feels like.

I lift her arm off my body and place it gently on the mattress. She doesn't stir. I stand, rubbing gunk out of my eye.

The man's body lies on his bed. His face still looks shocked. His mouth is open and his eyes are wide. I guess that's how he felt when he died. I don't imagine anyone is expecting their penis to explode; it must be an odd sensation.

I trudge toward the door, past posters of classic movies and some football medals on a set of drawers. Something on the drawers takes my attention. It's a photograph of the man and a woman. The man's arm is draped around her shoulders. I assume this woman is either an ex-girlfriend, or she doesn't know what he gets up to at night.

Or, at least, what he *used* to get up to.

I carry on to the next room. The flat is small, and only has two rooms—the ensuite bedroom, and the living room / kitchen. I find a glass from a cupboard—one of the few that aren't piled in the sink—and pour some water into it. I relish the feeling of water against a dry throat, and I look around the flat.

Something doesn't feel right.

There's a vase with some flowers in. A fluffy cushion on the sofa. Romance books on a bookshelf.

This doesn't feel like a man's flat.

And, just as the thought forms, a noise comes from the front door. It is a key in the lock.

Shit.

I go to rush back into the bedroom, keen to warn Pandora, but I pause in the hallway, wondering if I should hide instead, but why would I hide, whoever it is will hardly miss the penisless corpse of her boyfriend on the bed, I don't understand why he would have sex with another woman now anyway if she was due to come back but maybe they are polyamorous and—damn.

I've spent too much time dithering. She's entered the flat.

"Babe, I'm back from my trip early—my sister was doing my head in and–"

She steps into the hallway and freezes. Stares at me.

She has blond hair. Glasses. Wears a nice dress. Carries a suitcase. Pretty, and out of this guy's league.

Meanwhile, I am naked and covered in her boyfriend's blood.

She screams. Goes to run back out the front door, but I get there first and slam it shut. I lock it and turn back to her. She backs up. Goes to enter the bedroom.

Sees what's in the bedroom.

She screams again. The horror on her face is something to behold. She falls to her knees, covering her mouth, and I don't know what to do. I've barely spoken to women, never mind one who's just seen her boyfriend's mutilated corpse in a room decorated in his juices.

I run up to her, lift her to her feet, and put a hand over her mouth. I'm suddenly aware of my small penis flapping about. I press a handprint of her boyfriend's blood on her lips.

"Stop screaming," I tell her. "I will not hurt you—just please stop screaming."

Her eyes are wide and she's staring at me and she's not going to stop screaming because she's shocked and she's scared and she's terrified and I don't know how to calm her down–

"Please stop screaming, we don't want to hurt you."

She finally stops screaming.

"I'm going to let go of your mouth. Please do not scream."

I release her mouth. She doesn't scream. But she stares at me, her eyes still wide, her breathing speeding up. She flattens herself against the wall.

"Let's get you a glass of water, come on."

I grab hold of her arm and drag her into the kitchen area and place her by the door. As I fill a glass with water, I feel her eyes on my bare and bloody rear-end, and I wonder if maybe I shouldn't have left her by the door because she might make a run for it.

But she doesn't move. I imagine she couldn't if she wanted. People think our responses are fight or flight, but so often there's a third option—freeze. Her body is like a plank, and she doesn't take her eyes away from me.

I hand a glass of water to her. She just stares at me.

"Take it."

She doesn't move.

I grab her arm, lift it up, and put the glass in her hand.

She doesn't grip, and the glass drops and smashes.

"Dammit," I mutter, and wonder where their dustpan and brush are located.

Then again, considering the state of the bedroom, it probably doesn't matter.

"Would you like something stronger?" I ask her, and I open the fridge. There is beer in there. "A lager, perhaps?"

She still doesn't talk. Doesn't move. She is hyperventilating, and I'm worried she's going to pass out.

"You need to calm down, seriously."

Her breathing gets worse. Her eyes don't move away from me, and she's now wheezing.

"Look—can I pour you a beer?"

Still nothing.

I know how I look—naked and covered in puss and blood and bile and whatnot—but this is getting frustrating. She needs to hurry up and process it so we can figure out how to get out of this without her being hurt.

I lean against the kitchen side. Fold my arms. Consider putting some underwear on, but then I'd have to get past her and into the bedroom. Oh, this really is an awkward situation.

"So, quick question—do you have an open relationship, or was he cheating on you, because…"

I trail off. She's still not responding.

"Fine, I'll wait."

I sigh. Look around. They have the latest football magazine. I've never been too into football, but I enjoyed the England matches in the summer. I pick it up and browse it. Some man discusses a career he once had. It's not very interesting, so I put it down again.

She's still staring.

"Look, I think we need to–"

She screams.

"Fuck, stop it!"

She screams harder. Looks around. Uses the door frame to keep her steady.

"Stop screaming!"

It fills the flat. It makes me scared. What if someone hears her? What if we get caught?

"I need you to stop screaming."

I put my hands out to appear calming, but she doesn't stop.

"If you don't stop then—"

Then the screaming stops.

I take a moment to realise why, and it is not until she slumps on the floor, with blood pouring down her throat and Pandora standing above her, knife in hand, that I realise what's happened.

CHAPTER
TEN

I SHOWER.

Pandora goes to get the car, leaving me here with two dead bodies, and I stand beneath the forceful jet of water and I scrub and I scrub and I scrub and I try not to think about what just happened.

Pandora went from manic killer to business-mode so quickly, I haven't quite processed what happened. The woman had barely stopped spluttering by the time Pandora announced she was having a shower, then going to get her car, before instructing me to shower as well.

It's about a twenty minutes' walk to the hotel. Ten minutes to gather all our stuff and give the keys back. Five minutes to drive back with the car. And I have been standing under the water for most of that, unable to stop replaying the event over and over.

I use some shower gel I find on the side of the bath and run it over my body. I scrape off pieces of blood from my nails. Wash blood clots out of my pubic hair. When I finish, I step out and look in the mirror, and notice there is still some blood on my nose. I scrub it off with soap, get dressed, and walk into the bedroom.

The woman lies in the hallway. Arms spread out. Eyes following me around the room.

The man's body does not bother me. But hers…

It's because I'm innocent, isn't it?

I glare at her. "Shut up."

Make me.

I turn away. Look out of the window. The last stragglers of night life make their way home. The clubs have kicked them out, and they can barely walk. A man drapes his arm around a woman. They look as pissed as each other. I wonder how they'll feel in the morning.

Do you even know my name?

"I don't need to know your name."

I notice a photo frame on the floor. We must have knocked it off the bedside table during the excitement. I pick it up and place it where it belongs. The man and the woman stand with Mickey Mouse in Disneyland, beaming at the camera.

"Your boyfriend was a piece of shit."

He was my fiancé, actually.

"Whatever."

I knew he was cheating on me.

"Then why stay with him?"

Because I loved him.

"That's bollocks."

Are you telling me you wouldn't stay with someone you loved after they did something wrong?

The question lingers.

I look back at her. Her lips don't move. I don't know how she's speaking.

"That's different."

Why?

"Because she hasn't cheated."

But she killed me.

"She had to."

Why? What did I do?

67

"You… you were unlucky."

And I deserve to die for it?

"Enough!"

I look at the time. It's been half an hour. Where is Pandora?

I don't know why she told me to stay here. Perhaps it's because I still needed to clean up, and it saves time for her to remove our trace from the hotel then come back to get me. I'm not sure.

Heh, heh, heh…

"Oh, what now?"

Do you know if she's even coming back for you?

"She's coming back."

It would be awfully convenient for her to forget you…

"And it would be awfully convenient for you to shut up."

Make me — my words are all coming from your mind…

I sigh. I try to make them stop, but she keeps talking.

You really think she loves you, don't you?

"Shut up."

Are you really so lonely that you'll run away with a woman who–

"What do you know about it? You knew your fiancé was cheating, and you stayed."

How do you know I knew he was cheating?

"Because you told–"

No, she didn't. It's all in my head. I don't even know if they were engaged. Is there a ring on her finger?

She's killed an innocent woman now. Things have changed.

"I know."

You could run. You could do it now.

"What?"

You could get away. Maybe you could get a lighter sentence for turning Pandora in. Either way, this is the chance — leave the flat and run away.

I frown. "I love her."

Does she love you?

"Yes."

And you're sure?

"Yes."

You're not just lonely?

"Would you fuck off!"

I take the framed photo of them at Disneyland and I launch it across the room. It hits her head. She doesn't respond. Of course she doesn't, she's dead.

I just think you need to consider how much you can trust her.

"I can trust her with my life."

You can?

"Absolutely."

Because all it would take is one night of weakness where she climbs on top of you and pins your arms down and–

The lock in the door turns. It opens. Pandora steps inside.

"Are you ready?" she asks.

I nod. Glance at the body.

It doesn't say a word.

I follow Pandora out of the flat, and to the car parked outside.

SHE KEEPS IT INSIDE

She keeps it inside.

The rage. The hurt.

She keeps it inside.

She keeps it tucked away and safe, somewhere protected. Somewhere only two people could penetrate.

Her.

And Uncle.

Sometimes, *she* misses Uncle, and *she* doesn't understand why. *She* hates *herself* every moment a pang of loss throbs in *her* chest. What he did to *her* was abominable.

But the attention, and the closeness, and how special he made *her* feel...

It's hard to separate the man who made *her* feel so loved, from the man who did those things to *her* when *she* was just nine years old.

When *she* thinks back, *she* wonders why *she* never found it odd that he called himself Uncle, even though he wasn't a brother to Mummy or Daddy.

He was just Uncle.

The man with the kind eyes and the beard like Santa. *She'd* sit on his lap and he'd read *her* stories. Mummy and Daddy would go on what they called *date night* and Uncle would promise he'd keep *her* safe. He'd tuck *her* into bed and read *her* stories and tell *her* everything would be all right. There were never any monsters under the bed when Uncle was there.

He'd run his hand down *her* cheek and whisper that *she* was a princess. Like in Disney. And what did princesses do in Disney?

They kiss the prince, *she'd* reply.

He'd smile and say, well, go on then, kiss your prince, and he'd lower his face, pucker his lips, and *she'd* kiss *her* prince.

Then he'd say, do you know what else princes and princesses do?

She'd say, what, Uncle?

He'd say, never mind. He'd stand up. Put the book back on the nightstand. Say it's okay—you're too young to understand.

She'd say, no I'm not, I'm nearly ten, you can tell me; desperate to be old enough to know all the secrets.

He'd say he was worried that *she'd* tell Mummy and Daddy. That it's a big secret. That all adults know what princes and princesses do, and that *she's* not supposed to know, and that Mummy and Daddy would be mad at him if he told *her*.

She'd promise that *she* wouldn't tell, and he'd look upset, nervous, like he wasn't sure, and *she'd* insist and insist, no it's okay Uncle, it's okay, I'm really good at keeping secrets I promise I am I promise I promise.

Well, okay then. But it's not really something I can tell you. It's something I have to show you.

Then show me.

But it would mean you have to take your clothes off.

My clothes?

Yes, but it's okay, because I'll be taking my clothes off too.

But what if I'm cold?

Then I'll warm you up.

Okay, Uncle.

Actually, maybe I shouldn't.

What? Why?

Because Mummy and Daddy really won't want me telling you this. I'll go downstairs, you go to sleep, they'll be back soon.

No! Look, I'm taking off my pyjamas now, I'm ready, please show me. I promise I'll never tell. Never.

Never?

Never ever!

For as long as you live?

For as long as I live!

Okay, my darling. If you insist.

Yay!

Now, tell me, what have they taught you at school about bodies?

What about them?

Do you know what a penis is?

Er, that's like, what boys have.

Yes, exactly. Have you ever touched one?

Ew, no.

You mean, Daddy never let you touch his? Not even once? Not even just to see what it feels like?

Never.

Daddy won't like it if I do that then. Daddies are supposed to do it, so if he finds out…

I said he won't!

Okay, then I guess I better show you.

Right now?

Yes. Here. Have a look.

Is that it?

Yes.

It's big. And there are lots of hairs.

It's big because it's erect. Do you know what that means?

No.

That means that a prince is very excited by his princess. That's you.

Me?

You are the princess. And you are making your prince happy. That's what this means.

Oh.

It feels hard. Touch it, see.

It does feel hard. And there's a lot of skin.

That's called the foreskin—it's below the head of the penis because it's erect.

Oh.

But the penis needs to be kept warm. Nice and warm. Do you know what the best place to keep it warm is?

No?

There are two places.

Oh.

We will need to try both.

Why?

Because it's what princes and princesses do. You want to be a princess, don't you?

Uh huh.

Then we will need to try both.

Okay.

Open your mouth.

My mouth?

Yes. And close your eyes.

Close my eyes?

Do you trust your prince?

… Yes.

Then open your mouth.

Okay.

That's it. Good girl. Good little princess. Now open your legs. That's it. See what I'm doing with my hand, here? This is what makes princesses ready to make the prince happy. How does that feel?

(…)

How does it feel?

(…)

Are you a good princess?

Mmm… I… Ye…

That's okay, you don't need to talk. You just concentrate on what you're doing.

(…)

Open your legs wider.

(…)

See how happy you've made me?

Yes, Uncle.

Now lay down.

Yes, Uncle.

Feel that?

Yes, Uncle.

Now this is what princesses do for their princes. This is the secret.

Yes, Uncle.

And you will never ever tell anyone that I showed you this?

Yes, Uncle.

Good princess. Now let me show you how a prince and princess finish showing that they love each other.

Yes, Uncle.

Yes, Uncle.

Yes, Uncle.

Okay, Uncle.

Thank you, Uncle.

I'll never tell, Uncle.

Thank you for showing me, Uncle.

She bows *her* head.

Hides the rage. Hides the loss. Hides the memory.

Hides it as deep as *she* can.

She keeps it all inside.

All of it.

Buried away in a steel box with a combination no one knows.

Somewhere *he* can never touch.

She has no sympathy for anyone who gets in the way of what *she* keeps inside.

Even if it is another woman.

As *she* will not be deterred from her mission.

She will not.

She will not.

She will not.

CHAPTER
ELEVEN

The car ride screams with silence.

Everything that's not being said is an explosion between her in the driver's seat, and me beside her.

I go to speak on several occasions, then don't. I just let her drive. I don't know where we're going. At this point, I don't care.

Then I find the courage, and I am just about to say, "Why didn't you–" when she puts a hand on my knee and shushes me.

"Wait," she says.

I don't know what I'm waiting for. She's staring in the rear-view mirror, calm but alert.

I look over my shoulder. It's a police car.

I bow my head and close my eyes. This can't be happening. I can't let it. My future runs through my mind: my family's devastation, my face in the newspapers, my guilty sentence, my life in prison, being bullied in prison, and being raped by some beefy bloke called Butch McDick.

The police car's siren comes on.

I hold my breath.

We stop at traffic lights.

The police car swings to the outside lane, approaches us, then…

Then it speeds past.

It disappears around the corner, and the siren grows fainter until we can't hear it at all.

And we both breathe a huge sigh of relief. We even laugh a little, looking at each other with a happiness I haven't felt for most of the night. The sunrise highlights her beauty, and I forget why we were ever fretting.

"I love you," she says, placing her hand on the side of my head.

"I love you too," I tell her, and she kisses me, and it's electric, and I forget why I was scared.

Then I remember.

She stabbed an innocent woman in the throat.

She holds the kiss. The enjoyment leaks out of me, and I try to retain a performance of satisfaction as she takes her head away and leans her forehead against mine.

"I promise I won't ever leave you," she tells me.

I try not to gulp.

"Eric?"

I can smell her. It's hypnotic.

"Eric, do you promise too?"

"Yes… Yes, I promise."

The traffic lights change and she drives. She takes us onto the motorway, and we remain in a silence that feels more comfortable—at least, she seems to find it more comfortable. She even puts the radio on and starts singing along.

Then another police car overtakes us with its siren blaring and I'm not sure why, but the peace between us leaves again and she turns off the radio and she bites her lips and peers at the road.

After a few minutes, she takes us off the motorway, down a few country lanes, and we stop by a field.

"Get out," she tells me. It is not a request.

I open the door and step into the British countryside. In the distance, sheep graze the land. The surface is wet and uneven. She leads me to a river.

"Give me your phone," she tells me.

I feel for it in my pocket.

"Now," she adds.

I give her my phone. She drops it on the ground and stomps on it with her heel until it is just pieces of metal. She takes out her phone and does the same to hers, then she collects the pieces and hurls them into the river.

"Do you have anything else?"

"What?"

"An Apple Watch? An iPad? Another phone? Anything?"

"No."

"They are hunting us, Eric. The papers vilified Dave, but they won't vilify an innocent woman—there is going to be pressure on the police to find us. We cannot leave a trace."

She steps toward me. She's smaller than me, yet it feels like she's grown taller.

"That means your family, Eric. Every one of them. You cannot talk to them again."

I think of Mother. Of Father. Of how crazy they will go, how much money they will offer as a reward, how they will ring and ring and ring a phone that will never answer.

I think of my sister. Hiking up her skirt as she walks into the lunch hall and enjoying the attention she gets. She doesn't realise that she's a target, and I won't be around to teach her.

"Do you understand, Eric?"

I nod.

"Great."

She charges back to the car. Except, she doesn't get in. She locks the door. Then she turns back to me, folds her arms, and glares.

"Now why don't you tell me what the fuck is going on?" she demands.

I look around. There's no one here. There probably won't be anyone here for a while. We're in the middle of nowhere, and it's early in the morning, and the air is still fresh.

"I'm talking to you!"

She's so loud it makes me jump. Her statement reverberates through the open air.

"I—I don't know what you mean."

"I think you do."

"I – I –"

"Why don't you grow a set of balls and say it? Huh?"

She's crazy. She's scaring me. I don't know what she'll do. What is going on?

"I – I don't–"

"Come on, you know the words, you can say it."

I sigh. "Fine. I—I don't think you should have killed her."

She marches toward me. I don't have time to turn and run before she is in my personal space.

"And what would you have done, huh? Had a pleasant conversation with her? Reasoned with her? Explained what we are doing and got her to stay quiet?"

"I don't know. Maybe. Possibly."

"And you think that would work, do you?"

"I have no idea."

"Well, it wouldn't. Trust me, I'm not a naïve little child like you. I know how the world works."

Now that hurt. "That's a bit unfair."

"When have you ever been in a fight? When have you ever been abused? When have you ever had to look someone in the eye who's supposed to take care of you, and have them… have them…"

Her face scrunches up. She covers her face. Her body convulses as she cries. I try to put my arms around her, but she steps out of reach.

I don't know what to do. I've never had to deal with a crying woman before.

I try to hug her again.

"Pandora, look–"

"No!" She hits my arm away from her. When she lifts her head to meet my eyes, her cheeks are red and damp. "I am on a mission, and I thought you were on it with me too."

"I am."

"Then stop doubting me! Because they will not stop hunting us, Eric, and I will not stop. If you're not interested, then please, let me know, because I—"

I grab her arms and turn her toward me. "Pandora, I hate these men as much as you do. But she was innocent."

"There was always going to be collateral damage, Eric. It's a part of war we can't help."

I nod. Hold my hands in the air. "Fine. You're right. I'm sorry."

Her anger seems to drop almost immediately. The face of Medusa is replaced by the face of a sweet, innocent girl. Someone I want to hold.

"This would be so much easier if we could just have sex," she says. "If we could just relieve the tension with a good fuck, you know?"

Honestly, I don't. But I nod and say, "Yeah," as if I do.

"Come on." She takes my hand and leads me back to the car. I get in and she accelerates away. It doesn't take long before the tears are gone.

As she drives, I reflect on what she's just said. About looking into the eyes of someone who's supposed to take care of you. About being abused. And it makes me wonder how much I actually know about Pandora.

I know she's beautiful. I know she gets angry. I know she loves me.

But what happened before me?

How did she even get this ability? Is that even what it is? Is it a power—or is it an STI? Who gave it to her?

And, as I continue to wonder about all the things I don't know, I wonder just how safe I am.

She was nasty to me, though maybe I deserved it, and she had to make sure I did what I was told. But I love her, and I forgive her for that, I just wonder…

Would she ever make *me* fuck her against her will?

Would her craving for *me* ever get that strong?

And, should it happen, would I be able to say no?

LEVITICUS

SHE SEARCHES

She searches.

Only this time, *she* searches for something else.

Something for *him*.

Something to make *him* happy.

What's *he* even into?

She's the only woman *he's* ever been with.

Technically, they haven't 'been' together in terms of inter-course, and *she* knows that—but *she* also knows that what they have done together is far more intimate than any sex can be.

But *he's* still a man. *He* still wants sex. And *she* still wants to give it to *him*.

So *she* prowls the club. *She* doesn't tell *him* where *she's* going. *She* wants it to be a surprise.

This time, *she* is not looking for a man.

She is looking for a woman. Open-minded. Pretty. Possibly bisexual, depending on what *he* would like.

It feels odd, searching for a woman. *She* feels like a hunter, rather than a seeker, and *she* wonders if this is how men feel.

But *she* is not a man, and for that reason, *she* is sure *she* can get one. They will trust *her*. *She's* a woman. *She* is not a man searching for an easy target—*she* is like them, and so *she* is trustworthy, and so *she* can convince them.

She considers one woman. A sparkly silver dress just inches below her crotch. She wears a ring on almost every finger. Her earrings are large hoops. Her hair is blond, but not naturally. Her nail varnish is pink. Her lipstick is pink. The toenails in her open heeled platforms are pink.

Yuk.

She keeps looking.

She sees another woman. Black dress. Black fishnets tights. Black hair. Black lipstick. An expression like the world is awful, and it is everyone else's fault but hers. She sits with her arms folded and her legs crossed; her large, black boots thicker than her calves.

Does *he* like goth girls?

Possibly, possibly not. Either way, this woman's attitude is gross.

What about young girls? Does *he* like young girls?

Some men do, you know. And *he* doesn't have any idea how much *he* has in common with such men.

She keeps looking. Scouring the faces and the bodies. Searching for something that makes *her* excited; something that speaks to *her* libido, too.

And then *she* finds her.

A red-head. A short but modest dress. A subtle tease of cleavage. Natural makeup unnoticeably applied. Freckles that give her a youthful innocence.

And, what's more, *she* smiles.

So many of them don't smile. *She* understands why, of course—but a smile in the face of adversity shows character, and *she's* attracted to that character.

She makes jokes with her friends. Does silly movements. Dances like it's a bit of fun while those around her dance like it's their life's calling. Drinks Smirnoff Ice with a straw and does not leave her drink unattended. Shuns every guy who approaches. Has two rings, both complimenting her hand rather than making it look garish. She's come to this club for fun, not for a mission.

She reckons this woman is smart, too. And young. And open-minded.

She follows the target. Tracks her across the room. To the dance floor. To the bathroom, where women congregate. It's late enough in the night that the target will be a little drunk, but not so late that she can't stand upright.

"Hey," *she* says.

"Hey," the target replies.

And *she* explains the situation.

CHAPTER
TWELVE

My parents are on television. Both of them sit at a table in between police officers, with flashes of cameras going off every few seconds. Mother is crying. Father has an arm on her back, and is keeping it together. He believes that being strong for your family means showing no emotions. I don't.

"Eric, we ask you, please come home," Mother says as she dabs her eyes with a tissue. She usually keeps one up her sleeve. "Please. We don't care what you've done, we know you're being made to do things, and we know it isn't you. Please, just find an opportunity to escape, and come back to us. We promise you will be safe, and you will be protected."

Mother's emotions become too much to handle, so Father takes over. I hate how much they play the parts handed to them by patriarchy.

"Son, if we have done anything to upset you, we are sorry. We know this is out of character, and for that reason, we are concerned. Your university is happy for you to continue once you return, and the police are here to listen to your story, not judge you. You are with someone who is going to mislead you, who is going to do bad things, and who is not being completely honest about why she's with you. Please, just find your opportunity to escape, and take it."

The lock to the hotel room turns, and I quickly turn the television off with the remote. Pandora walks in. She looks amazing—like she's been to a club.

And she has a woman with her.

A red-headed woman. And their arms are around each other. And they are giggling. They seem a little tipsy.

"What's going on?" I ask.

The red-head stumbles toward me, pushes me down, and crawls on top of me.

"You must be Eric," she says. She smells like vodka and cigarettes. "Pandora has told me so much about you."

I look over the woman's shoulder at Pandora. "What's going on?"

"This is Tiffany," Pandora says. "She wants to meet you."

Tiffany grins. I can see down her top. Her tits are tiny and perky. I'm turned on, but confused. She kisses me and I push her off.

"Woah, no, no—I'm with Pandora," I tell her.

Pandora sits on the bed beside me and holds my hand. "It's okay. I brought her for you."

I look between them, perplexed.

"Pandora told me about your situation," Tiffany says. "That you can't have sex, because Pandora has to abstain before marriage, but that you need–"

"Woah, no, hang on—that's not why she can't–"

Tiffany puts a finger on my lips and shushes me. "Just relax. I know you're a virgin, it's okay–"

I push her off and leap to my feet. I'm angry, but I'm also aware that my large erection propping up my trousers is making Pandora chuckle at my annoyance.

"What are you doing?" I ask.

"What do you mean?" Pandora says. "I felt bad that you weren't having sex, so I thought—"

"That you'd go pick up some random woman from the club to have sex with me?"

"Well, yeah…"

"And you think that's okay?"

"I don't understand. I thought you'd be pleased."

Pandora stands. She smells of vodka too. It makes me feel queasy.

"What on earth would make you think I'd be pleased?"

"Because you get to have sex!"

"I don't just want to have sex, Pandora! Funnily enough, I care who I lose my virginity to."

"Really? Still? I thought you'd be eager to–"

"Then you were wrong."

An awkward silence descends. I expect Tiffany to leave. She doesn't. She lies on the bed, looking around the room. She sighs, like this is boring her, and she wants to get on with it.

"Eric, I don't get it. I'm offering you a chance to have sex with a hot woman. Most guys would jump at a chance to—"

"If I was like most guys, then you would have fucked me already, remember?"

At first, she looks confused. She tries to figure out what I mean. Then it dawns on her that this isn't what I want. But it still doesn't compute. After all, I'm a man—why wouldn't a man want this?

And she really, truly cannot see why.

She thinks she needs to entice me. That she needs to make me feel more comfortable about it. That it's a matter of reassuring me it's okay, she won't be upset. So she lies on the bed with Tiffany and runs a finger up her body.

It's like a scene from a porno movie, and I know most guys would kill for this moment—but it feels wrong. I feel like I'm cheating on Pandora, even if she's not only giving me permission, but is asking me to do it. I don't think I can physically have sex with this woman. It feels like a mistake.

And I feel scared.

And the thought of sex terrifies me.

I don't know what I'm doing. I don't know how to put it in or what to do with my hands or what to say or what to think or how to move. Everything about it makes me freeze.

I try saying this to Pandora, but she's kissing Tiffany. Just like how she kisses me. And it doesn't turn me on—it makes me feel jealous.

This isn't a man she has to fuck to kill. This is a woman she's choosing to seduce.

"Pandora…"

She beckons me onto the bed. Even takes my hand and tries to pull me closer. She's undressing Tiffany, and Tiffany is in her bra, and it's purple and lacy and it's sexy, but it feels immoral, like I shouldn't see that, because I want to be faithful to Pandora.

I don't want to sleep with just anyone.

I want to sleep with the woman I love.

And I can't take it anymore.

So I leave. I charge out the door, march into the car park, and stop by the road. It's raining hard. It drenches my body within seconds. The wind is howling and I feel cold, but I don't care.

I crouch.

I don't know why, but I crouch.

I run my hands over my head, missing the hair Pandora made me cut off. Water drips into my eyes, and the rain makes it hard to tell if I'm crying.

What am I even doing here?

Am I an idiot?

Is she taking advantage of me?

And what did my parents mean when they said that Pandora would mislead me? What do the police know?

I sit on the pavement for half an hour, feeling the water bombard my skin. I lean my head back and relish it. My sister loved the rain when she was a kid. She would see the raindrops fall and immediately insist that we go out on our bikes, or kick a football around the field; anything to get wet and muddy.

Now, she refuses to go out if it's so much as spitting for fear that it will ruin her hair or smudge her makeup.

At some point, Pandora sits next to me. I don't notice her walking over, and she says nothing when she joins me.

After a few minutes, she puts her hand on my hand. I don't respond. She asks, "Is this okay?"

I look at her. Try to show her my tears before the rain washes them away.

"I'm sorry," she says, and moves closer, and rests her head on my shoulder. She takes hold of my hand in both of hers. "I shouldn't have just assumed you wanted to do that. I just want to have sex with you so much, and I know you never have, and I just thought…"

"Well, you thought wrong."

"I know. Most men would want to, and I just didn't even entertain the idea that… I don't know."

"I'm not most men, Pandora."

"I know that. I do. She's gone. You don't have to worry—she won't be coming back."

I accept her apology and leave it there—although her last sentence stays with me. I'm not sure why.

She won't be coming back.

Did she mean that, as in, she won't be coming back because she's left and knows in no uncertain terms that sex will not happen?

Or, as in, she won't be coming back because Pandora has done something to her?

I shake myself out of it. Assume it's the former.

Of course it is.

Why wouldn't it be?

What could Pandora possibly have done to her?

NUMBERS

CHAPTER
THIRTEEN

IT IS FIVE DAYS LATER, AND PANDORA IS TAKING A SHOWER IN preparation for another evening at the clubs in pursuit of our next target. I am watching the news, half-watching stories about politicians and millionaires and all the things they've done wrong, when a news report starts that makes me feel sick.

It is a report of a man whose penis has exploded.

This shouldn't be surprising—we've gone through quite a few men now, each one as satisfying as the last.

But this man is in Hull. We have never been to Hull. We did not do this.

I consider whether Pandora could have done this, but there is no way. When I wake up in the night—which happens a few times—she is still there. We spend all day together. We don't leave each other's side for the hours it would take for her to go to Hull, find a target, fuck that target, revel in that target's remains, then drive a few hours back again.

The police do make an arrest, however. A woman, who they subsequently let go, claiming that there is no way they could link her to the succession of similar deaths across the country. What's more, they have found an internal infection. An infection she didn't know about. Which means she did this to the man involuntarily—if she did it to him at all—and she is now in hospital, being quarantined and examined.

A news reporter interviews a medical spokesman.

"It would appear that she is carrying an infection that behaves much like an STI," he says. He has a brown suit and a grey beard. He looks like he would make a lovely grandfather. "We believe that this is a new virus, and it appears to be dormant in women, as it does not affect the X chromosome. When we added a Y chromosome to the infected blood, however, the reaction was quite something."

"What happened?" asks the off-screen reporter.

"Well, it caused the blood to expand, and keep expanding, until the blood exploded and ruined my microscope."

"Exploded?"

"Exactly that."

I peer through the crack in the bathroom door. The shower is still running, and Pandora is singing a song from a musical I recognise but can't place. I move to the edge of the bed and lean toward the television.

"So how is the infection passed on?"

"Again, we are very early in our research, but we believe that this is a sexually transmitted infection. However, seeing as the infection is proving fatal in a man, we believe it can only be transmitted when a woman has sex with another woman. Any woman who has both male and female sexual partners will be at a much higher risk of transmitting the infection."

"But, just to clarify, a woman doesn't need to worry? Only men?"

"That's correct."

"Should we not advise men to watch their behaviour, then?"

"Oh, absolutely. Men should undoubtedly avoid dressing

to attract attention, or getting too drunk, or being out too late. And they should stay in groups, just in case. A woman may not be able to control her urges, and they may find that they end up getting hurt."

I run my hands over my face. How did someone else get this STI? Did they get it by the same means that Pandora got it?

"And these other cases of men receiving similar fatalities —do you think they are being deliberately targeted?"

"Oh, yes. Very much. Men, especially in night clubs, need to watch their drinks carefully, need to make sure they use contraception, and need to make sure they do not encourage a woman's behaviour. Men need to be very, very careful not to warrant unsolicited attention from a woman, as they may well be carrying this infection."

They cut to the newsreader. "The woman who is believed to have infected the latest victim remains in quarantine, and has so far declined to comment, but we were able to speak to her father today."

A man with a large moustache appears on the screen.

"My daughter would not hurt anyone. The men are lying. I don't know how they got hurt, but I know who my daughter is, and I resent that they are trying to ruin her life with these accusations. Tiffany is a kind girl."

Hang on.

Wait.

What did they say her name was?

I glance at the door. The shower's still going.

I turn the television down and lean closer.

"The woman in question, Tiffany Spelling, is said to be in a stable condition."

A picture of Tiffany Spelling appears on the screen. She is in the middle of her family with arms around her siblings, whose faces have been redacted.

Tiffany has red hair.

Freckles.

She looks a little different in daylight and without makeup, but it's her.

It's definitely *her*.

The shower stops.

I change the channel. Some music video is on where a man with chains around his neck is jigging to a hip-hop beat whilst spouting lyrics about hoes and whores.

Pandora leans around the bathroom door.

"Why on earth are you watching that?" she asks.

For a moment, I think the news is still on, then I realise it's the rap video. "I, er… just trying to be down with the kids, I guess."

"If there is one thing you are not, Eric, it's down with the kids!"

She returns to the bathroom, chuckling, and starts drying her hair.

I stare at her figure through the crack in the door. The buttocks. The curves. The dangerous beauty. The woman no man can resist. And I wonder…

Did she know she was transmitting the infection to Tiffany?

Did she do it by mistake, or did she have sex with her in that half hour between me leaving the room and her coming to find me, deliberately, to pass it on?

Is the woman I love a hero taking revenge, or a psycho aiming to torture all men out of some deep-seated hatred of my gender?

And if it's the latter, how safe am I?

She walks out of the bathroom in her underwear and opens the cupboard. "Which dress do you think?" she asks.

I stare at her with my mouth open.

"Jeeze, you'd have thought you'd have seen my body enough that you won't be speechless anymore. Do you really find me that attractive?"

I stutter over a few syllables.

"Men!" she scoffs, takes a dress, and returns to the bathroom.

And I sit here, staring at the space she just left, reminding myself that I love her. And that I trust her. And that she's never hurt me.

I mean, she's been forceful. A little aggressive. Gone behind my back.

But she's never actually done anything to show she'd hurt me.

Right?

CHAPTER
FOURTEEN

WE GO THROUGH THE SAME PROCEDURE AS NORMAL. SHE WALKS down the street, and I lag behind, watching as drunken groups of lads aim catcalls in her direction.

I've spent each night pitying those men. Thinking that any of them could become the target. Knowing they do not know the power of the woman they are messing with.

Now, however, I feel sorry for them.

I don't know why.

Perhaps it's because they are all so pathetic.

They are young. Engaging in group mentality. Thinking they know who they are, but in truth, having no idea. They are, what—nineteen, twenty? Their identity is yet to be decided. They make stupid decisions now, but for all we know, when they grow up, have children, fall in love, they may reflect on their behaviour and regret it.

Then I follow her into the nightclub, and it feels like a giant cesspool of toxic lust. The place stinks of pheromones.

I do not know what pheromones smell like, but that's how it stinks.

The women wear their short dresses, and the shorter the dress, the more men feel entitled to her. Those men strut around like apes or peacocks or puffer fishes, trying to impress the opposite sex, and it's all so silly, isn't it?

The males establish a hierarchy. The alpha leads the pack. He tries to woo the wayward female.

And if the female doesn't buy into what he's offering, he simply hits her around the head with his club and drags her into his cave.

Pandora looks back at me. She's dancing in the middle of a group of men. Each of them thinks they have a chance. She wants me to pick a target. I hadn't been paying attention. I'm supposed to pick out the one who's been acting the most inappropriately throughout the night, but I've been distracted. I'm failing in my duty to her, and I need to pull my finger out of my arse and concentrate.

I notice one of the group of men leering at another woman. He walks past her, rubbing his hand across her cleavage by 'mistake.'

I point to him. She nods. She makes the approach, and he's all too happy to dance with the eager female.

The alpha has chosen its prey.

But who is going to penetrate whom?

She dances up against him. Kisses him. It used to make me excited. Then it made me want to scream. Now it makes me scared.

It doesn't take long until she's whispering in his ear, then he's nodding at his mates who nod back, sticking out their bottom lip at his perfect catch, and he drags her outside so quickly that I have to run to keep up.

He takes her to a flat above a sandwich shop. I wait a moment, then enter. I walk up the stairs and through the corridor. The floor is uneven and the wall curves over me. The smell of rotten sandwiches from the store below fills the building.

The door to the flat is ajar. She is already grunting her fake sex noises. I push it open. It creaks a little. There is a kitchen I can barely stretch my arms in that leads to the door to the bedroom. There's no living room. This poor guy can't even afford a proper flat.

I look over the dining table as I wait. Although 'dining table' is a loose term—it's a small garden table that you'd struggle to fit more than one person around. It used to be silver, but most of the surface has come off, and it is mostly black.

There are textbooks piled on top of it. I pick one up, then another, reading the names. *Medical Physiology. Clinical Anatomy. Becoming a Medical Practitioner.* Beneath them is a leaflet about applying to the NHS.

Holy shit, this guy is training to be a doctor.

Her grunting comes to a crescendo, and his grunting gets harder. I feel like telling her to stop, but it's too late now. I consider running out the door, but fear what she would do to me if I did.

So I stand and listen. They both finish. She gets up and the floorboards creak. He talks: "Where are you going, baby? That's only round one."

It doesn't take long until the screaming starts.

Followed by him running around. Going crazy. Terrified. Realising his own mortality. Attacking his own penis.

Then there goes the exploding flesh.

A few minutes pass. There is sloshing around. She's enjoying herself already.

"Eric?" she calls.

I sigh. I need to go in. I know I do.

I glance back at the textbooks, then enter the bedroom.

The bedroom is as sad as the kitchen. A single wardrobe. Dark red walls—not in a sexy way, but in a crumbling-unable-to-afford-to-repaint-them way. This guy's skint because his money is going on his medical education.

At least, it was.

"What's the matter?" she asks, lying beside the body on

the bed. She waves her arms around the blood like she's swimming, then rolls over and slides onto the floor, where more blood awaits her.

"Come on!" she says. "You're missing out!"

I feel queasy. I don't know why.

"Eric, are you coming?"

I gulp.

"Eric!" She sits up. Glares at me. "What the fuck are you doing? Come on!"

"Pandora, I'm not feeling too good."

"What the hell do you mean, you're not feeling too good?"

"I mean, I feel sick."

"Fuck off, Eric, you're not the one who had to fuck this bastard. His cock smelt and everything. I did that for you—so now we are going to enjoy it."

"I can't."

"You can't?"

"I'm sorry, I–"

I turn to go. She stands, rips the guy's alarm clock out of the wall, and launches it across the room. It collides with the door, inches from my head.

I stay completely still.

"Pandora, please don't make me."

"Don't make you? I did this tonight, and I did it for you. I paid to get in, I paid for drinks, and I rode this guy so his dick explodes. You even chose him. You owe me this."

"I don't–"

"You *owe* me."

I bow my head. I don't want to, but she's pretty insistent.

"Come over here."

"Please, I–"

"Now."

My body droops. I turn to her. I think about all the things I would say if I were to stand up to her, but none of my objections meet my lips. I trudge slowly forward.

"Stop."

I stop. "What?"

"You're still wearing clothes."

I look down. I don't feel like getting naked. "Pandora, please–"

"You *owe* me this, dammit!" She punches the wall. Plaster crumbles. My arms are shaking.

I take my top off. My shoes. My trousers. I hope that's it, but she raises her eyebrows and I remove my underwear too.

"Now get on the bed."

I get on the bed.

"Bend over."

I bend over.

She grabs the back of my hair with her right hand and drags the corpse closer to me with her left.

"I want you to put your head in the hole."

"What? But I've never–"

"I didn't ask."

Her hand is strong against the back of my head. The gaping wound where the man's genitals once presided opens toward me. The outside of the wound consists of red gunk and tissue, like a pothole in the road, but instead of cement and puddles it's skin and blood.

I lower my head to it. Feel my forehead stroke the top of the wound, ending just beneath his navel, as my chin strokes half of a scrotum that hangs off the opening via a flap of skin.

"More."

I lower my head in more. Close my eyes. Place my face against it. It's soft against my skin. Sticky, but soft.

"More!"

She shoves my head and presses my face harder against his insides. I feel something long and gunky and stinking like faecal matter and I'm pretty sure it's his large intestine. It unravels around me like a cobra. Urine leaks from half a bladder that rests against my forehead.

"Lick it."

I open my mouth. My tongue runs upwards. It feels like mud coated in sugar, and tastes like shit and piss. I stick my tongue into something, and I'm pretty sure it's the inner opening of his rectum.

She pulls my head out. Looks at me. Admires a face painted in a stranger's bodily contents. She shoves her tongue into my mouth, licking up what I licked, then runs her lips over my face, ingesting everything that sticks to my skin.

I sit still, allowing it to happen. I don't say no, so I guess I deserve it. I allowed this to happen. My lack of objection is my act of consent.

Once she's done, she takes the corpse's head, holds the body over the floor and jiggles it, forcing its contents to fall out like a bag of sweets.

So many bloody items land on the floor, and I can't tell what most of them are.

She lifts something up. A piece of intestine, maybe? A clump of blood vessels? It's squidgy yet hard. Liver, perhaps?

"Eat it."

I don't want to.

But the look in her eyes stops me from objecting.

I've already gone this far. I've already agreed to do so much. I may as well continue.

I eat what she tells me to.

When we are done, she uses a pair of scissors from the bedside drawer, cuts out the corpse's tongue, and sticks it inside of herself. I think she was planning to masturbate with it, but it ends up getting lodged too far inside, and she can't get it out again. I panic, but she finds it funny, and after sticking a few fingers up there, she queefs and it falls out.

She laughs at it. I try to laugh too.

Then we shower together, like usual. Like nothing's happened. She runs her hands down my body to help remove all the gunk and blood and bits of flesh and unrecognisable items that cling to me, then she does the same to herself.

We drive home in silence.

Then she says, "I really enjoyed that, didn't you?"

I turn to look at her. There are no streetlamps, and her face is in shadow. Her smile looks ominous in the darkness.

"I really like it when you're submissive," she says. "We should do it again sometime."

She puts her hand on my leg. I used to think it was an affectionate gesture, but now I think it's to claim me—to assert her dominance.

I don't push it away.

GOVERNMENT GUIDELINES

Following the death of a man in Hull, we can confirm that this death was caused by a sexually transmitted infection given to him by a bisexual woman, who is now in quarantine. Medical scientists have investigated the infection and are prepared to issue the following information.

How it Works

The presence of the infection introduces parasitical bacteria into the body, which expands haemoglobin that is present at the same time as the Y chromosome. As the testosterone levels increase during an orgasm, and the presence of the Y chromosome becomes more apparent, the haemoglobin cell begins to expand. At first, this will cause the head of the penis to swell and become painful. Those showing signs of infection may be tempted to strike the swelling to quell it, but this will only exacerbate the issue.

Within 10-50 seconds, the haemoglobin will have expanded to such a level that the head of the penis will reach the size of a balloon. The presence of the bacteria will also generate a large quantity of puss, which, along with the blood, will also make the penis expand. Eventually, the penis will explode under the strain, and the impact of the explosion will cause interior organs to rupture, and also potentially explode, meaning that a fatality is highly probable.

Symptoms

The infection is asymptomatic in females and, for this reason, we cannot test to see if it is present. The parasitical bacteria does not reveal itself until the Y chromosome is present—meaning that, in females, the symptoms will not present themselves.

As for males, you will not show any symptoms until shortly after sexual intercourse—somewhere between 10 seconds and 2 minutes. By then, it is too late to combat, and will most likely prove fatal.

How it Spreads

As any man who has this infection will die within minutes, it is not possible for a man to spread the virus. However, a woman can spread the virus by having sex with another woman.

We do not believe that the virus can spread through oral sex alone, but that vaginal juices must be directly exchanged. Any women engaging in an act of rubbing their vulva against another woman's vulva will significantly increase their risk of catching it.

How it Can Be Cured

The first hurdle with curing it is identifying it—and, as the infection does not present itself without the Y chromosome, and does not grow until testosterone levels increase, we cannot identify its dormant presence in females.

This means that, without sufficient quantities of the infection, we cannot provide sufficient research into a cure.

It is worth nothing that this is not just bacteria—it is parasitical bacteria. The parasite needs both a penis and a Y chromosome to grow. As it is a parasite, it is more intelligent than your average bacteria, and will have greater defence mechanisms against vaccines and attempts at destroying it.

Ultimately, there may be no way to cure this, and condoms are not strong enough to protect yourself against it. We advise all males to be cautious when engaging in sexual activity, and to ensure they do not attract non-ideal attention from females.

CHAPTER
FIFTEEN

WITHIN HOURS OF THE GOVERNMENT ADVICE BEING ISSUED, THE news is reporting that masses of women are actively seeking to get infected.

Women, who see the infection not as a burden, but as a defence mechanism against the unwanted attention of men, seek bisexuals and lesbians to engage in sexual activity with them. Friends who haven't shown any homosexual inclination before exchange vaginal juices with each other in an attempt to catch the virus.

Men claim this is extreme feminism, and that it is an attack on their gender.

Women claim it's protection, and that it is to ensure that any man who takes advantage of them when they are alone, or drunk, gets the consequences they deserve.

As the infection spreads, women act more liberally. They dress as they want; they go out and act as they wish; they dance as sexily as they crave, and they don't bother monitoring their drink.

Men go to clubs in groups, if they go out at all. They protect themselves from the opposite sex. They do not walk alone at night, for fear of being sexually assaulted or molested, and incurring the infection.

Pandora pops out for an hour, here and there. She says she's just going for a walk. Then she comes back to the hotel with her hair in a mess, and she has this little smile—this sneaky, half-grin, where one side of her mouth lifts and the skin beside her eyes wrinkle.

"What were you up to?" I ask.

"Oh, not much," she says, and she goes in the shower.

In the days that follow, more and more incidents of penis explosions occur. The news stops reporting individual cases and starts reporting statistics. Men speak out about how they are going to the police about women harassing them and making them feel unsafe, only to be told that no crime has taken place. They cannot prove a woman has made them 'feel uncomfortable' and are advised to just avoid attracting unwanted female attention.

I go along with what Pandora wants me to do. I love her, but a lot of her requests get more and more extreme, and make me feel increasingly uncomfortable—I find myself regularly sticking my head inside the corpses, eating parts of the body I don't want to eat, and penetrating myself with parts of the body I don't particularly want inside of me.

As difficult as this is, I don't even entertain the notion of another life than this. I'm addicted. I crave her. Whenever she is mean, she redeems herself with an act of kindness, and I know she's not that bad. And, when it comes to playing with the bodies, any resistance I give just turns her on. She loves it when I play, even though I'm not playing.

A few weeks pass, and reports of the police searching for us fade from the news, and I wonder if they are still after us.

But they must be. As far as they are concerned, Pandora is ground zero. She was the first, and will be most likely to have the answers they seek.

And, one evening, as we watch a film about giant worms,

I gather the courage to ask the question I've been wanting to ask for a while.

"Hey, Pandora."

"Hm?"

"You know this infection?"

"Mmhm."

"Where did it come from?"

She shrugs.

"Surely you must have some idea?"

"Why does it matter?"

"Because you are the first. It started with you—surely you must know?"

"Why would it matter if I did?"

"Because... I don't know. It's spreading. And maybe it would help cure it."

"Why would we want to cure it?"

"Because innocent men are dying."

"Innocent?"

"Yes. It's not just men we're targeting who are in danger anymore—this is all men. If they have sex, they risk what will happen."

"I'm okay with it."

"You're what?"

"I said I'm okay with it."

"But what about nice guys? Guys like me?"

She turns to me. Smiles like I'm a child asking a stupid question. Rubs her hand down my face and pinches my cheek.

"Oh, Eric," she says. "There are no nice guys."

"I'm a nice guy."

She gives me that smile again. I don't know what it means.

"Then you're one of a kind," she eventually says.

"How can you know that for sure?"

"Every time I so much as speak about what happened when I was a child, there will be a man who'll say 'it's not all men.' And do you know what I do? I test that man. I get drunk and see what he does. And every time—every damn time—it turns out he *is* one of those men."

There are so many arguments I have. The limits of anecdotal experience, the fact she's only tested this hypothesis on a handful of men—but I don't argue with it. There is something else she's said that distracts me. Something I'd never figured out before, yet seems so obvious.

"What happened when you were a child?"

"What?"

"You said when you speak about what happened when you were a child—what happened?"

Her smile goes. She shifts her body. Almost recoils away from me.

"Nothing," she lies.

"Pandora, it's me. You can tell me."

She turns to me. Gazes into my eyes. Like she's trying to size me up. Like she's figuring out who I am, and whether I am 'not all men.'

"I wasn't a child for long," she says.

"None of us are children for long–"

"No, Eric. You got to be a child for eighteen years. I was nine when my childhood ended. I hated sex before I even knew what it was."

"Who did this?"

She remains silent.

"Who, Pandora? Maybe we can go to the cops, tell them who it is, and they can—"

"You have so much faith in the police, don't you?"

"Why wouldn't I?"

"Because you've never had to talk to them about…"

She looks down. I can't tell what she's thinking. Until now, I've had her figured out, but she looks like a stranger to me. She looks weak. And she doesn't want to look weak, so she forces a smile.

"That's it," she says. "That's all there is to it."

"It sounds like–"

"That's it, Eric. I know what men are like. Trust me, I know."

"It's not all men, Pandora."

She says nothing. She turns back to the movie. A giant worm is wrapping itself around a woman and eating her head and, even though Pandora's eyes focus on the screen, it feels like she's elsewhere.

And I wonder… how long until she decides *I'm* like every other man?

How long until her love for *me* isn't enough?

She feels detached. Separate. So disconnected. I say nothing else about it, hoping not to push her away. Hoping that she will return to herself soon.

When the film finishes, and the news starts, she goes to the bathroom and locks the door.

I mute the television, not wanting to hear about how many deaths occurred yesterday. The figure keeps growing, and it's already enough. If a man can't walk down the street without feeling safe, then the world has become a scarier place than I could have imagined.

And it's all because of *her*.

SHE CRIES

She cries into the sink.

She feels pathetic.

This is what the weak female character does, isn't it?

She never shouts, *she* screams. *She* weeps at the first sign of emotion. *She* requires a man to save *her*. Such an emotional being, such a complex gender, such a fucked-up world where we're taught who we are from birth; blue or pink, Barbies or Action Men, delicate or aggressive—it's all predetermined, and it's all bullshit.

Oh, shut up, *she* tells herself. You're going on again. You're always going on.

They deserve it.

They all do.

But does *he*?

She stops crying.

She won't cry.

He is *her* salvation.

He is a signature of faith, a promise of what the world will become if all evil men are gone.

But evil men always look so much like the good men, don't they?

That's because they think they are good. The evil man never sees what makes them evil. They can't reflect upon their own behaviour and pick out the hypocrisy. And, after all, it's *not all men.*

'Not all men.'

Pah!

Do you know how many times *she's* heard 'not all men'?

She almost hates *him* for saying it. It's a phrase that sparked the anger *she* needed to begin *her* crusade. It was enough to light the rage inside of *her*, the one that craves vengeance, the one that craves justice—the one that craves blood.

It's been so sadistically erotic to have *him* dance on the blood of the demented with *her*; to have *him* rejoice in the decoration of the damned; to have *him* celebrate in the death of those who wronged *her*.

But *she* mustn't forget who *he* is. *She* mustn't forget *her* mission.

Because of *her*, the world is changing.

Women in the world are claiming their power.

Men have claimed that *she* uses *her* sexuality as a weapon, and *she* supposes that it's finally true.

Fuck it.

She straightens *her* back. Wipes *her* eyes. *She* will not be dissuaded by *him*. *She* will not be reasoned with, will not be deterred, will not be talked down to. *He* will not force *his* male logic on *her*.

He will not mansplain how men are suffering from misinterpretation.

He will not.

He will not.

He will not!

She punches the wall. *Her* fist hurts. *She* doesn't care. Men punch things when they are angry and no one says a damn thing—*she* can do the same.

It's so funny, how the men who say 'it's not all men' always turn out to be one of those men.

She remembers Gerald.

Twenty years old with a small goatee. He was in a band. They played punk music at the local pub and her friends thought he was a god. Truth was, his band's music was poor, and he worked at the local restaurant as a dishwasher. He would rant about immigrants and how they wanted to steal his job. *She'd* wonder how they'd take his job if he was doing it well, but *she* never said it.

To *her*, this man was perfect.

To him, *she* was a naïve fourteen-year-old girl.

Her periods had arrived later than most. *Her* breasts were still small, and *she* was barely out of a training bra. But at that age, you fancy an older man. You think it's just taboo. You think it's just frowned upon, and something you should keep secret. *She* always saw teenagers having affairs with their teachers in soap operas, and he was nowhere near as old as *her* teachers. Besides, it was only six years—if *she* was thirty and he was thirty-six, no one would say anything, right?

At that age, one doesn't realise that it's abuse. Or that it's not just taboo, but that it's illegal. That it's not just romantic lines or courting or charm or one of the unrealistic romance movies perpetuated by Hollywood—that it is, in fact, *grooming*.

She didn't know that he laughed with his mates about it.

She didn't know he knew he shouldn't be doing this.

She didn't know that the words *I love you* didn't make *her* feel special because he loved *her*; they made *her* feel special because *her* childhood had equated love with abuse. They were the same thing.

She'd sit in his flat while he watched porn or played on his PlayStation. Sometimes his mates would come around, and *she'd* have to move off the sofa to make room for them. *She* didn't care. *She'd* just enjoyed having a boyfriend.

None of *her* friends had boyfriends. *She* was special.

Then his friends would go and he'd tell her to strip off. *She'd* ask if he'd kiss *her* first and he'd huff and he'd stomp over and give *her* a kiss and ask why *she's* being so needy.

She'd lie on the bed like a rag doll and he'd give *her* cunt all of his cum.

Sometimes, he'd get her so drunk *she* couldn't stand, and *she'd* wake up unable to remember the night, shocked to discover *her* inner thighs were sticky.

That's what sex is, right?

You just lie there while the guy does what he needs.

Then he'd leave *her* alone so he could go play his guitar or watch rugby with his housemates or drink beer and smoke weed in the garden. *She'd* lie on the bed, semen dripping out of *her*, considering whether *she* could switch his television on or whether he'd be mad when he came back up. *She* was cold in a house where the heating was never on, but didn't know if *she* should put her clothes back on yet. *She* didn't want to upset him.

When *she* reached fifteen, *she* grew a self-awareness *she* hadn't had before. *Her* breasts were fuller and *her* hips were more pronounced and *her* mind was latching onto all the things wrong with this world.

She missed Uncle, and often thought of him, and wondered where he was; but *she* didn't try to find him. *She* had someone else to grab *her* waist and smack *her* arse.

One day, *she* told Gerald that *she* wanted him to kiss *her* during intercourse. He laughed. Then he fucked *her*. He went to turn *her* over, and *she* said *she* wanted to look at him. He told *her* to shut up and turn over, and *she* said please, let me look at you. He became angry and said turn over and *she* said maybe I don't want to do this and he turned *her* over and grabbed *her* hair and shoved *her* face so hard into the pillow that *she* couldn't breathe and *she* wondered if *she'd* die.

She would love to say *she* stood up to him. That *she* left in a moment of courage. That *she* realised what he'd done was wrong, and *she* was strong and that *she* told someone *she* trusted and that the arsehole was convicted.

In truth, Gerald grew bored with *her*. His text messages grew less, and *her* visits became less welcome. He faded from *her* life with no objection from either party.

She'd looked Gerald up a few years ago. He wasn't in a band any more. He was a teacher. Head of Physical Education at the local comprehensive. He had a Twitter account where he frequently posted pictures of feminist quotes that he disliked with the hashtag #NotAllMen.

But now *she's* grown up. *She's* found *her* voice. *She* uses it, and does not care what anyone thinks of its volume—and now *he* wants to tell *her he* is suffering and that it is not all men and that *he* is a good guy, waiting out there in the bedroom, scared to voice his opinion. Oh, no, the angry feminist will disagree and then *he* will have to explain how the world works to *her*, oh la de da—*fuck you*.

Fuck all of you.

They have voiced their opinions, and *she* has had to listen.

No more listening.

No more clutching *her* keys when a group of lads walk past *her*.

No more flinching when a man catcalls *her* from a van.

No more guarding *her* body from molestations in the nightclub.

She has only just begun.

And now the infection is spreading, and more women are claiming it, and more women are taking revenge, and *she* has started something beautiful and it is only just beginning.

Who's hysterical now, huh?

Who?

She turns back to the door.

He's on the other side.

Sitting there, with *his* firm belief in what is right and wrong.

Sitting there, with *his* condescending looks and *his* reasoned arguments.

Sitting there, sitting there, sitting there, sitting there sitting there sitting there sitting there and fuck *you* for condescending to *her*.

Is *he* the exception?

Are there any exceptions?

She hasn't met one yet. Why does *she* think *he's* different?

He loves *her*.

He says *he* loves *her*.

She believes *he* loves *her*.

Maybe *she* should let *him*. With caution. For now.

Ready for the moment *he* removes the mask and reveals the cretin beneath.

That's when *she* will pounce.

And that is when *she'll* be proven right.

CHAPTER
SIXTEEN

I MISS MOTHER AND FATHER.

I don't want to miss them. But I do. I miss talking to my sister, and sharing my day with my parents, and telling them about what I'm studying, and what I'm planning to do once I graduate.

And I need to hear their voices.

It's not that I want to leave. At least, it's not that I'm planning to, I should say. I just can't get rid of the image of them on the news; they really seemed to care. They were adamant I should escape. But escape what?

I stand. Edge toward the bathroom door. I know I'm not supposed to go out, but I won't be going far. Just outside. Just to use the phone.

I tap my knuckles lightly on the door and listen for a response.

"Pandora?"

She says nothing.

"I'm just popping to the vending machine to get a chocolate bar. Would you like anything?"

Still nothing. But I hear movement. She's definitely in there.

"I'll be back in a few minutes."

I back away, staring at the door, expecting her to burst out and slam me against the wall and demand to know what I'm up to.

But she doesn't emerge. And I'm able to walk out of the door, take a brisk walk across the hotel car park, and pause outside reception. I ask the receptionist if he has a phone, and he points to a phone box outside.

It's in full view of the room. If she looks out of the window, she could see me.

I consider whether to risk it.

I put my hood up. Turn away from the room. Hope she won't notice me in the shadows of the night. There isn't a single lamppost, and the darkness conceals me well.

I only have a few coins in my pocket. I place them in the phone, and it gives me just over a minute. I take a deep breath, press 141 to make sure the number is blocked, then dial my parent's number.

It rings. And rings. And rings.

Then someone answers.

"Hello?"

"Father?"

"Eric, is that you?"

His voice makes me feel like crying. I wasn't expecting how much turmoil I'd feel; it's a mixture of sickness and relief. My body is already tense, and it stiffens even further.

"Eric, are you okay?"

"I'm fine. I—I just wanted to hear your voice…"

"Where are you? Tell me and I'll come and get you?"

I shake my head. Rest my head against the receiver. Glance over my shoulder at the room, checking the curtains aren't twitching.

"I'm fine, Father. Really, I'm safe. You don't need to get me."

"Eric, you don't understand, the woman you're with—she's not safe."

"She's perfectly safe."

"No, she isn't, she has a history of domestic violence and–"

"That's not who she is now. She's changed."

"Son, I–"

"I don't want to talk about Pandora!"

I hate that I snap at him. I check how much time I have left. It's not much. I don't want a lecture; I want comfort.

"I just wanted to say…" What? What did I want to say? "That I'm fine. That you don't need to look for me."

Father mumbles something. It sounds like he's talking to someone else.

"Father, who is that?"

"What? Oh, your Mother."

He's lying. There's a man's voice whispering.

"Are the police there?"

"Listen, Eric–"

"For Christ's sake, Father, I wanted to talk to you."

"Eric, you don't understand, I know this woman."

"I know you think you do."

The time is almost up. I go to tell him I care for him. That I love him. And Mother. That I'm okay.

But he interrupts me with his final statement.

"Eric, you need to listen to me, Pandora is—"

And then he cuts off.

Just like that.

I place the phone on the receiver. I hope blocking the number was enough to stop them finding it. That the call didn't last long enough to be traced. The last thing I want is for police to show up here.

I put my hands in my pockets and trudge back to the room. When I enter, Pandora is sitting on the edge of the bed.

The lamp lights half of her face. I can't tell if she's been crying.

She stares at me with an intensity that makes me feel like I've done something wrong.

"Are you okay?" I ask.

"Where's the chocolate bar?"

At first, I'm confused. Then I remember where I told her I was going.

"Oh, I, er… I ate it."

She stands. Strides toward me. Kisses me. Not romantically, but with force. Her tongue is stiff and deliberate.

I realise she's checking my mouth for the taste of chocolate.

I wait for her to accuse me of lying. But she doesn't.

"Come to bed," she tells me, and climbs under the covers. I get in next to her. She turns away from me and waits for my arm to nestle around her.

"I love you, Eric," she whispers.

Her hair rustles against my head. The curve of her body fits neatly against the curve of mine. My wrist rests between her breasts, and I feel them against my arm. It should feel good. I don't know why it doesn't.

"I love you, too," I tell her.

She turns out the light.

PROVERBS

CHAPTER
SEVENTEEN

WAKING UP EARLY IS A SHOCK. IT'S USUALLY APPROACHING lunchtime by the time we get out of bed. Why not? We mainly perform our activities at night, so it's not like the mornings would be particularly productive if we did get up. Besides, neither of us are morning people, and lying in bed with my arm draped over her has been the perfect way to wake up for the past few weeks.

Not today.

I stir, and I'm immediately aware that the other side of the bed is empty. I turn, feeling for her, unable to find the familiar curve of her body. I glance at the alarm clock. It's barely eight. Where is she?

I sit up. The toilet flushes. I assume she's just woken up to use the bathroom, but when she re-enters the room, she's dressed. Her hair is tied back, she has modest earrings in her ears, and she wears a vest and jeans.

She never dresses like this anymore. It's always provoca-tive—at least, provocative in the way a predator might see it. Short dresses, large hoop earrings, long hair. Not because she's trying to attract attention during the day—but because she can. She doesn't fear male attention anymore, knowing what she can do.

But today feels different. Not only is she dressed more casually, but her movements are also swift and hurried. She's tidying up the room and shoving stuff in our bags.

"What are you doing?" I ask, rubbing my eyes.

"Get ready," she tells me.

"Get ready?"

"Yes."

"Where are we going?"

"Just get ready, and I'll show you."

She picks up my t-shirt and jeans. Throws them at me. I catch them and await further information, but none arrives. She carries on gathering our things.

I do as I'm told.

Ten minutes later, I'm dressed and ready to go, craving a coffee.

She says we don't have time for a coffee and tells me to get in the car. I consider arguing or questioning further, but she's carrying our bags to the car before my tired mind finds the words.

Once we are in the car, she drives, and she drives with purpose. She spends the entire motorway journey in the outer lane, speeding past every other motorist. We go north, and we keep heading in that direction, her eyes fixed ahead with such determination that I become too scared to ask what we are doing.

I turn to the window. Watch cars go by. Couples with kids on the backseats frown at us. I close my eyes, but she hits my leg and tells me to wake up. Says that she doesn't want me to sleep. I ask if I can put some music on to keep me awake, but she tells me no. She doesn't look at me.

She finally takes us off the motorway as we approach Manchester. She doesn't take us into the city centre, but directs us toward a housing estate. We approach an area full of run-down houses, where blokes walk down the street taking large swigs from cans of lager, and teenagers get rowdy as they hang around on the street corners; one of whom flips the bird at us.

She brings the car to a halt beside a large row of terraced houses. She gets out of the car and waits, tapping her foot as I take too long to follow her. She walks to the front door of one of these houses and, instead of knocking, walks right in.

She turns and glares at me. "Hurry up."

I move from a stride to a brisk jog, and follow her inside.

A short woman walks up to us, late fifties with short, scruffy hair and loose-fitting clothing. I think her arms are shaking a little, but that just might be my tired mind trying to adjust.

"Can I help you?" she asks, then looks at Pandora and says, "Pandy?"

"Stella!" Pandora says, opening her arms and enveloping the woman in a bear hug.

The woman—Stella, apparently—glances at me.

"How can I help?"

"This is Eric." Pandora looks at me, but without the same warmth she gives Stella. "I'd like to educate him, if that's okay?"

Stella nods. "Anything for you. Claire is in room one, she'd be up for talking."

"Thanks, Stella, you're a star."

She stands back and allows Pandora in. Pandora reaches for me, and I think she's going to grab my hand, but she doesn't—she grabs my wrist and pulls me in.

She takes me to the first door. It's open. A woman sits by the window. She is so thin that, at first, I'm not sure if she's real. Her skin clings to her bones. Her right cheek is swollen.

"Claire?" Pandora says.

The woman jumps and turns around. She's missing teeth. "Yes?"

"Do you mind if we come in and talk to you?"

"Okay."

Pandora walks in. Claire recoils as I enter, but calms down when Pandora says, "It's okay—he's safe." Claire glances at me once, then doesn't make eye contact with me again.

Pandora sits on the edge of the bed. She shoots me a look that I assume means I'm meant to do the same, so I do.

"How are you?" Pandora asks. Her voice is far quieter and far more nurturing than I've ever heard it. I wonder why I never see this side of her.

Claire shrugs her shoulders. Sighs. "Okay."

"Be honest."

"I—I'm waiting for him to turn up. I didn't tell him where I was going, but he could find me, and I'm just sitting here, looking in the windows of all the cars that go past, checking to see his face, and…"

She trails off, then stares at her feet.

"Who's *he*, Claire?" Pandora asks.

"My husband."

"Surely you'd want to see your husband?"

Claire shakes her head. She opens her mouth to reply, but nothing comes out.

"Do you have children?" Pandora asks.

Claire nods.

"How many?"

"Three."

"Where are they?"

"In care."

"How come?"

"They said the home wasn't safe while he's around."

Pandora nods. She places a hand on Claire's leg. Claire stares at it at first, wary of being touched, then forces her lips into an unconvincing smile.

I huff, and I can tell this annoys Pandora. I get the point. I get why she's brought me here. But did she really think I wasn't aware that places like this exist? Did she really think I didn't know that some women are treated like this?

What is she trying to achieve?

"Pandora, I'm going to wait in the car."

I turn to go. Pandora stands, stomps her foot, and I halt at the door.

"I don't think we're done yet," she says.

"But I–"

"We have about, what, twelve women here?" She looks at Claire, who nods. "And I want to meet them." She steps toward me, scowling. "That's right, Eric. Twelve women. *Women.* Not a single man among them. Why is that?"

"Because men are arseholes?"

"Are you being clever?"

"No, I just don't get the point. And I want to go."

"Fine. Go."

I walk out. I hear her thank Stella as I shuffle out of the front door. Once we're outside, she charges toward me and shoves me against the car.

"Don't you ever embarrass me like that again," she says. "Do you hear me?"

"Pandora–"

"That woman is fragile, and I wanted to talk to her, and I think you needed to hear it."

The curtain flickers. I notice Claire watching us out of the window. Pandora doesn't—she sets her glare on me. It's intense. I feel like it's my fault Claire is in there.

"You seem to think I don't know–"

"You don't. Clearly. The way you were questioning me yesterday, it was like you've completely forgotten what we're doing."

"What we're doing? Pandora, I thought we were having fun. I thought we were hurting men who deserve it, then doing… whatever it is we do… together."

"Yes, but there's also a point. If we are going to do this on a larger scale—"

"What larger scale? You're creating a world where no man is safe, whether or not he is innocent."

"And you think any of them are innocent? That they've never spoken to my breasts instead of my—"

"Jesus Christ! Have you never checked out a guy's body? Looked at his arse? You're acting like every man deserves this!"

"And they don't?"

"I don't, Pandora! *I* don't!"

I let the statement linger. It seems to settle over her, dripping down her body like rainwater. I finally think I'm getting through to her.

I put my hand on her arm, and add, "Who is it that hurt you, Pandora? Who is it?" And again, this seems to get through to her, and she bows her head, and a flicker of pain crosses her face. She is Pandora again, and she is no longer mad at me, and I am no longer the source of her anger.

Which is why I wish I'd left it there, instead of saying what I say next.

"It's not all men."

Any sympathy she had for my argument fades, and it fades quickly. She is glaring again, and she is shaking her head, and her hands are gripping into fists and her arms are quivering.

She is furious, and I am scared of her.

She marches to the driver's side of the car. Grabs the door and pulls it open. I think this is it—that it is over. That I'm going to go. That our relationship, if that's what it even was, is through.

Then she says, "Get in the car," and I know that it's not.

I look at her for a moment. The moment doesn't last long, but it is the moment where a large, complex set of thoughts unravels in my mind.

Once it ends, I get in the car.

And I know I will look back at this decision as the turning point—as the moment where I set the rest of my life in motion. It is what people refer to as a 'sliding doors moment'—one where I will wonder what would have happened if I hadn't gotten in the car.

I can predict that, without a doubt, *you* are asking why I don't just leave.

And if you even ask that question, then you can't understand why.

But I will explain.

There are two reasons.

The first: addiction.

I am addicted to her.

She has times when she is nasty. Vicious. Abusive, even. Times when she demeans me and doesn't allow me to have my opinion and makes me feel worthless and treats me like a sexual slave.

But it's redeemed by the loving side, where I do feel safe, and I do feel wanted, and I do feel nurtured.

I crave that side of her. I need it. Just as a heroin addict can't stop injecting their arms with toxic crap, I can't help but fill my body with her.

I depend on my fix of Pandora to keep myself high.

And then there is the second reason.

And this is a far stronger reason than the first.

It is fear.

I am terrified of her.

If I leave, will she find me?

If I go to the police, could they do enough to protect me?

If I tell other people, will they understand, or will they say, "Oh, but she seems like such a nice person?"

Truth is, I'm ninety-nine percent certain that she will find me, police will not protect me, and that no one will believe me.

If I leave, I can never sleep. She will find me and fuck me in my slumber. I will wake up to fireworks above my balls.

I know there is no escape from her. To even try would be futile. I am terrified of being hurt, should I ever make her unhappy. My life is now a constant mission to ensure that she never becomes resentful enough to make me feel her wrath.

So I do up my seatbelt. I shut up when she tells me to shut up. I let her choose the music.

And we drive to wherever she decides.

SHE WAS ONLY EIGHTEEN

She was only eighteen by the time *she* feared the world.

Or rather, by the time *she* feared men.

She wore short dresses. *She* sent guys *she* liked pictures of *her* breasts. *She* flirted when a man offered to buy *her* a drink at the bar. *She* went to clubs and danced and gyrated *her* hips and laughed and had fun doing it.

To them, *she* was signalling *her* sexual availability.

And, hell, this may have even been true—*she* wasn't averse to the odd hook-up—but, if *she* was signalling *her* availability, it was a signal to the *right* man; not *every* man.

She needed self-esteem. Male attention was the way to get it. They looked *her* way and peered down *her* top and scanned *her* legs and admired *her* smile, and it made *her* feel like *she* was worth something.

Uncle had taught *her* that *her* worth was measured in sex.

Gerald had taught *her* that *her* worth was measured in sex.

And every man *she* encountered once *she* was freed from the shackles of childhood—once *her* parents no longer constrained *her* to the house on a Friday night—reinforced that *her* worth was measured in sex.

She didn't want a man to save *her*, but *she* wanted a man to tell *her she* was worth more. That *she* didn't need to find confidence in the bed of a stranger. That *she* didn't need to find *her* self-esteem in the attention of perverts.

But *she* never met that man.

She was only eighteen. *She* was subject to *her* experiences. *She* did not know better.

She sought wisdom in other women and they all told *her*, over and over, you are most likely to be killed by a man; you are most likely to be oppressed by a man; you are most likely to be hurt by a man; most likely to be objectified; overlooked for promotion; a man is more likely to abuse a child; abuse a teenager; discard your feelings; abuse power; discard the notion of consent; commit evil, atrocious acts.

It turned out to be true. When *her* friends weren't finished in the club, but *she* was tired and wanted to go home—when *she'd* had *her* fill of attention—*she'd* have to leave by *herself*. *She'd* walk down well-lit streets, and *she'd* be terrified by the instances other women had warned *her* about.

A man in a van honking his horn at *her*.

A group of lads cat calling.

A man walking too close behind.

A man crossing to her side of the street.

She'd seek groups of women and walk behind them, as if they would keep *her* safe.

But *she* was never safe.

They didn't have to touch *her* to make *her* feel disgusting. It was in a comment. Or a look. Or proximity.

She was only eighteen, and all life had taught *her* was that *she* was in danger. That all men could hurt *her*. That all women were in danger. Constantly.

She stayed scared.

Then *she* grew angry.

With everyone.

A man staring at *her* on the bus would be met with a spew of shouting and hostility.

A man arguing with his wife on a park bench would have *her* hands on his throat and words in his face that made it clear that if he spoke to her like that again, *she* would make him eat his own cock.

A man who walked past *her* in the street and told *her* she should smile more would find *her* hand on his testicles, squeezing like they were stress balls; and when he told *her she* was a crazy bitch, *she'd* pull and pull, then *she'd* pull harder, and he'd beg *her* to stop

She would not take any more shit. No man would fuck with *her* again. *She* would ruin the life of any man who made *her* feel uncomfortable.

Men would have to fear walking alone; men would have to watch their behaviour; men would have to fear a woman's sexual dominance.

She schemed.

She planned.

And *she* seethed.

She was only eighteen, and it was years until *she* would meet Eric, and it was years until *she* would begin *her* crusade —but the pieces were there.

She had already become a monster.

GOVERNMENT ADVICE

The Prime Minister announced this morning that he has assigned Jennifer Grey to the recently created government role of 'Male Protection Minister', a role created to act on fears of men that our society is becoming an increasingly dangerous place to be. Despite outrage from male rights campaigners that a woman has been granted this role, she has vowed to do what she can to help end male suffering.

Shortly after news of her appointment, she released the following statement:

It is with great honour and a deep understanding of the situation that I accept the role as Male Protection Minister. Recent events have shown a rapid growth in the as yet unnamed sexually transmitted infection that is seeing detonation in many male appendages, and I am committed to making the world a better place for men.

As such, we have conferred with the police, and are offering men the following advice for a safe night out.

1/ Safety in numbers. Remain in large groups and avoid leaving anyone on their own. By remaining with people you trust, you will reduce the risk of being targeted by females who wish to take advantage of you.

2/ Use taxis. I am aware of recent stories about some errand taxi drivers who have taken advantage of their male customers—but please be assured that this is incredibly rare, and riding in a taxi is still a safe, viable way to get home. When you are in the taxi, ensure that you sit in the back. It may be a little more expensive than the bus, but you will be less exposed to attention from the opposite sex.

3/ Always book your taxi in advance. Using a service means there is a track record of your journey and will provide you with extra security.

4/ Drink in moderation. If you are inebriated, women are more likely to take advantage of you. Many drunk men give consent without remembering it the next day. If you are not sober enough to be in control, then you can expect a woman to see you as an easy target. Similarly, ensure you keep your drink covered, otherwise you may give a woman an opportunity to put something in your drink.

5/ Use well-lit areas. People are less likely to commit an attack, or to harass you, if there is decent lighting or CCTV. Plan your route home to avoid canals or alleys, as you may make yourself an easy target.

6/ Dress appropriately. If you go out with too many buttons of your shirt undone, or wear shorts that reveal too much of your legs, women may get the wrong idea. By sending women signals that you are available, you are putting yourself in a position to warrant unwanted attention.

7/ Keep away from hostile situations. If there is conflict, or you see someone else being harassed, don't be a hero. Stay away, and contact bouncers or the police if you feel the need.

Let's make sure that we behave in a way that keeps us safe and does not give a female predator the opportunity they are after.

CHAPTER
EIGHTEEN

THINGS IMPROVE.

I do as she asks, and she seems happier.

She still goes out at random times of the day, the news still reports that infections are spreading through the female population, and more and more men are falling victim to the nasty effects of this lethal STI.

But we're happy.

Honestly, we are.

I remember how it was in the beginning, exciting and new, and I know if I just do as she asks, we will go back to how it was. Happy, smiling, cuddling during the night and taking pleasure in each other's company.

I don't necessarily agree with her plans. That's fine. Couples don't always agree. Are we a couple? I think we are, though we've never mentioned it. It's hardly like we're monogamous. Well, on her part, anyway. But that's part of the war she's waging. A war I'm part of. She's passionate about it, so I support her passions.

This is what you do to make a relationship work.

Father always told me—it's impossible to have a good relationship without bad times.

Some days, we have the bad times. She's stressed out, or angry, or on edge, and I just have to be careful not to upset her, or give her cause to turn her fury toward me. If I upset her when she's in this kind of mood, then it's my fault, really, and I should be more careful.

Is it always easy? Hell, no.

Is it worth it?

For her, yes.

Because when she's not angry, and not shouting, and not telling me where to go and what to do and what to wear, she is sweet. When she stares into my eyes, runs her hand down my cheek, makes my body shake, causes my heart to quicken, and tells me she loves me—it's worth it.

I avoid putting the news on when she's in the room. It makes her angry. And it's probably sensible—I know it will cause an argument. They report how many men have succumbed to the STI, and it perturbs me, as I don't know which of those men deserves it, but I say nothing as I don't want to make her mad, and having the news on just draws attention to the tension between us whenever the topic is brought up. So I have the volume on low when she's in the bathroom, and turn the channel over as soon as I hear the toilet flush or the shower turn off.

On this particular day, she has been in the shower for a while. I lie on the bed, watching a woman on the news report on the deaths, and I can't help but feel like this reporter is trying to hide a smug smile. They interview men, each stating that they don't feel safe anymore, and feel especially worried when they walk past large groups of women, who always seem to stop and stare at them.

Women don't seem to care. When interviewed, they make comments such as, "Well, they should smile more," or, "They should be flattered," or, "If they dress like that, then they are asking for it."

One particular woman stands in front of the camera with a

lecherous look on her face, like she knows something we don't. She chews gum with her mouth open.

"It's funny, though, ennit?" she says. "I mean, all I have to do is make a comment—in fact, not even that; I just look at them, and they well-up like I'm going to attack them. They fear me, and they don't even know why."

The shower turns off. I change the channel. Some female rappers on the music channel are strutting around, miming the words whilst scantily clad men dance behind them.

The door opens. Slowly. Pandora stands there, an arm draped against the doorway. She wears a small, skimpy nightie, red with laced edges. It props up her breasts and reveals her long, smooth legs. She tries to entice me with her eyes, widening them, smiling.

"Hey," she says, her voice sultry, smooth like silk.

"Hey…"

She saunters toward me, swaying her hips, and pauses by the bed. She places a foot next to my waist, revealing her inner thigh. She isn't wearing underwear.

"What's up?" I say, and hate myself for how I sound. I just don't know what to say.

"I want to try something," she tells me.

"O… kay."

She climbs onto the bed. Sits over my legs. Unbuckles my belt.

"What are you doing?"

She shushes me. Removes the belt and throws it across the room. Unbuttons my trousers and pulls them down my legs, then dumps them on the floor.

"Take your top off."

"But I–"

"Now."

I take my top off.

She removes my underwear with her teeth. She grins when she sees my erection.

"I still don't understand what–"

She puts a finger over my lip. "Shut up."

She places her mouth around my penis. It feels good. Should we be doing this? Can she transmit the infection orally?

"Pandora, I don't think we should do this."

She ignores me. I can't stop her. This has never been done to me before.

After a few minutes, she stops. Sits up. Licks her lips like she's enjoying it. I don't know if she's actually enjoying it, or whether it's part of the act. She climbs up my body, then hovers her crotch over mine.

"What are you doing?"

She takes my penis in her hand and guides her vagina toward it.

"Pandora?"

Its tip reaches the opening.

"Pandora, what are you doing?"

I put my hands against her body to push her off. She doesn't move away, but hovers, holding my penis, waiting to put it inside of her.

"Are you trying to kill me?"

She shakes her head. "I think I can control it."

"What?"

"I was thinking about it last night—I reckon I can control it. Stop it from happening. Choose who I give the STI to."

"You can't choose, Pandora."

"I really believe I can."

She sinks lower, going to put me inside of her, and I push her away again. "No! Stop!"

"Don't be such a prude."

"It's not safe!"

"I said I can control it."

"How do you know that?"

"I just think I can."

"I said no!"

I push harder. She feels strong. I'm struggling to keep her away.

It's difficult, as I want to do this so badly. I want to know what it feels like, and I want that intimacy with her, and I want to find out what it is men are so desperate for.

She wants it too. She seems to take my erection as consent. Like if I didn't want to, then I wouldn't have an erection.

"Pandora, I don't want to risk it."

"There's no risk."

"Pandora, stop!"

She lowers herself, and I begin to enter her.

I push her away as hard as I can, then roll off the bed and dive onto the floor. I back up against the wall, putting as much distance between me and her as the perimeter of the room allows.

She lies on the bed, her head resting on her hand, laughing at me.

"Bloody hell, Eric, I didn't realise you were so scared. You just need to relax, it will be fine."

"I don't want to risk it!"

She shrugs. "There's no risk. I know I can control it. And I know you want it."

I'm shaking. I didn't realise it, but I am. My whole body quivers. Tears accumulate in the corner of my eyes, and I fight them as best as I can, desperate not to reveal how she's making me feel.

"Come back to bed," she says. "Come on."

I shake my head. Wipe my eyes. Look downwards, ashamed.

She stands. Walks toward me. Crouches in front of me. Laughs again.

"Please don't," I whimper. "Please, please don't… I don't want to…"

"But you do want to."

"No, I can't… I don't want to catch it… I don't… Please…"

She scoffs. "You are pathetic."

She stands and saunters back to the bathroom. She doesn't close the door; she sits on the toilet, staring at me as she pisses.

I don't meet her eyes. I don't feel I'm able to. I am humiliated. I am embarrassed, but I don't know why.

She puts pyjamas on. Sits on the bed, whilst I stay huddled up against the wall, staring at her. She flicks through the channels on the television until she finds some wrestling. She watches it, heckling at it every now and then.

She knows I'm still here, but it's not like it matters. I'm ignored. Just a part of the room. She doesn't seem to care that I am scared and stupid and barely a man.

Eventually, she turns to me, and she rubs the empty side of the bed whilst saying, "Come to bed."

I get up. Shuffle over. Sit down.

She puts an arm around me and pulls me close.

"You know I'd never hurt you," she tells me. "There's no one else in the world like you."

The words soothe me. I feel warm again, and comforted, and safe. I cuddle up to her as she watches a bunch of men in leotards dive over each other. It's not what I want to watch, but I leave it. She seems to enjoy it.

And that's how quickly we return to normal, though my mind festers on the issue, despite her seeming to have moved on.

Is it my fault?

Am I not supporting her well enough?

Should I be a bit more understanding?

The thoughts fade, and the noise of the television grows distant, and eventually I fall asleep, feeling content in her arms.

ECCLESIASTES

CHAPTER
NINETEEN

She insists, and she keeps insisting, that she can control it.

But it's almost like she doesn't care if she can't.

It doesn't affect her. She wants something, and so she will say all the right things to make me give it to her. And I know that, eventually, she will just take it, whether I agree to it or not.

So I tell her to prove it.

She says fine. She hatches a plan. When we go out, and we find our target, she will tie him up so I can enter and watch her fuck him, and she will control it, and she will not make that man's penis explode.

I hesitate. Consider what my life has become, now we are negotiating the politics of her capabilities to avoid a penis exploding. Then I agree.

And so here I am, standing outside the house of some sleazy bloke she picked up in the club. He's tall, chubby, and ditsy. He stood on the dance floor for most of the night, swaying from side to side, staring intently at nothing specific. He grunted when women walked past, and sometimes followed them, as if unable to control his orientation.

The front door is open. I enter. A pile of grubby shoes are pushed against the wall, each welly or trainer separated from its pair. I walk along stained floorboards on the stairs, each step prompting another groan. The whole place smells like weed and body odour.

She grunts. He grunts.

She grunts harder, and I wonder how a man can't figure out that it's fake—then I wonder if the man cares.

The bedroom door is open. The man lies on the bed—the sheets of which are crumpled, dirty, and display the Manchester United crest—with his arms bound to the headboard via handcuffs and his ankles bound to the railings at the bottom of the bed.

She's naked on top, moving her hips back and forth. I can see his balls below her buttocks. For the first time, this repulses me. I am no longer thinking of the pleasure we will gain by sharing in the remnants of his body, but am instead imagining what she will do with the remnants of mine.

Her eyes are closed, her face pointed toward the ceiling, like she needs to use her imagination to maintain enough arousal to keep going. The waddle of his throat sways from side to side as he stares at the perky breasts of the woman that straddles him, his eyes wide as if he can't quite believe his luck.

Then his head rolls to the side, and he sees me.

He screams. He goes to get up and seems to forget that he's bound to the bed.

She shushes him, places a hand over his mouth, and says, "It's okay. That's my boyfriend. He likes to watch."

I feel warm inside when she calls me her boyfriend.

"I didn't agree to that," the man grumbles.

"He won't bother us."

She continues riding him. After looking rather disgruntled, and shooting a glare in my direction, he returns his gaze to her naked body.

Evidently, my appearance is so unthreatening that he's not even bothered I'm here.

Pandora turns toward me, smiling as she moves back and forth, back and forth. It's so bizarre to watch. I've seen it in porn, and now I've seen it live, yet I still haven't even done it myself.

"Cum for me," she tells him. "Please cum for me."

He thrusts into her—as much as he can without being able to use his arms and legs. He thinks she wants his cum. Truth is, she's bored, and she wants it to be over already.

She increases her screams, makes them louder, more frequent, an Oscar worthy performance, and he grunts harder and she makes high-pitched chirpy noises that sounds like a bird is being whacked with a tennis racket, and he cums and she (pretends to) cum and then she rests there, on top of him, her hands pressed against his chest.

She leaves him inside of her for a moment, then turns to me and says, "The moment of truth."

He looks confused.

She dismounts him, steps away, then takes a clump of tissue from a tissue box beside the man's computer and wipes away his semen as it dribbles down her legs.

Then she stands by me. Takes my hand. And we both watch the naked man, bound to the bed. His pot belly sticks out, his penis shrinks until it disappears amongst the forest of his pubes, and he looks perplexed.

"You gonna untie me?" he asks.

Neither of us moves.

"Hey, you gonna untie me or what?"

She huffs. I wait.

"Oi, don't just stare at me, untie me!"

He pulls on his restraints. The bed rattles, but he's unable to liberate himself. He pulls harder and gets more agitated, but we ignore it, waiting for the effects.

A minute goes by. Then another. Then another.

And with each passing sixty seconds, my jaw drops a little bit more.

She was right. I can't believe it.

She can control it.

"Can we fuck now?" she asks me.

"Nearly," I tell her. I just want to be sure.

The man screams. Then he realises no one is coming, and he begs. We stand here, just waiting, and ignoring everything that comes out of this idiot's mouth.

And, indeed, his penis does not explode.

She turns to me and says, "See? I wouldn't lie to you."

I smile. I feel so stupid. How could I have ever doubted her?

"I'm sorry."

"Now take off your clothes."

I go to remove my top, and she takes over, pulling it up, hurrying me. I undo my belt and my flies and she pulls down my trousers and underwear. I look weird wearing nothing but socks, but she shoves me onto my back before I can take them off.

"Finally," she whispers, kissing me, pressing my body against the coarse surface of old carpet. "I've waited for this for so long."

"Me too."

I really have.

Twenty-six years, in fact.

"What the fuck are you doing?" the guy on the bed asks, amongst many other things—by this point we have tuned him out.

She puts me in her mouth to get me hard—but she doesn't have to suck it for long. I am raring to go. I am excited, aroused, ready, eager, desperate to finally bloody do this!

She sits over me. Grins.

"Are you ready?" she asks.

I nod. I feel nervous. My belly flutters.

It hits me: Oh my god, I'm actually about to have sex.

I'm actually about to see what the big deal is.

She takes hold of me and guides me toward her vagina—which I am grateful for, as I have no idea how to find it. The tip strokes the opening.

She lowers herself onto me, and I enter her a millimetre at a time. She does it slowly, to tease me, and it makes me even more desperate for her to just ride me.

Then the bloke on the bed makes some weird noises.

"Ignore it," she tells me.

She sinks lower.

Then he makes louder noises. Splutters and screams. Then he lifts his crotch into the air, screaming harder and harder.

I put my hands on Pandora's hips, stopping her from lowering herself any further.

"What?" she asks. "What are we waiting for?"

The man moans, "My dick… My dick…"

"I said to ignore him," she says, and lowers herself further.

I grip harder on her hips to stop her.

"What's the fucking problem?" she says and strikes my chest. "Stop pushing me off—I want to have sex!"

"Please, I–"

"I asked politely, now take your hands off my hips."

But the bound man on the bed is screaming harder, and his bellend is glowing with the orange parasite, and it grows larger, expanding behind Pandora.

I immediately push her off and scarper backwards until my back meets the wall.

The man's dick grows bigger, and bigger, and we say nothing.

I see it all in my periphery, because I am staring at her, and she is staring at me. I can't read the look in her eyes. I don't know if it's disappointment or annoyance, or her simply thinking *you dumb fuck*, but I don't like it.

She almost had what she wants, but now the guy's dick is expanding, and she doesn't seem to realise why we still can't have sex. It isn't a potential death to her—it's a mild inconvenience.

Neither of us reacts when the guy's dick explodes. Blood and puss and excrement spray over us like someone's just driven through a puddle of this man's bodily juices. Pieces of skin land on her face and on my body, but we say nothing—we do not even move.

Then, as the man stops struggling and his body falls limp, she shakes her head—a small, seething movement.

She bows her head. Huffs. Then stands.

It only takes several seconds until there's a smile on her face again.

"Fine," she says. "Now, what shall we do with this guy?"

She turns to the guy and runs a finger around the edge of the open wound, then sticks her finger in her mouth like she's tasting cream.

I stare at her, not moving from my place on the floor. She doesn't seem bothered that I'm not joining in. She has fun with the guy by herself—sticking her fist inside of him and licking up the excess blood and pulling pieces of muscle tissue apart and licking the inside of his torn bladder and smearing the contents of his intestines across her breasts.

It doesn't matter that I'm not partaking in what we normally do together.

It doesn't matter that I'm huddled into a ball, staring at her, still in shock, still not knowing what to do or say.

As I watch her, I understand something that I couldn't seem to understand before.

I have to leave.

I have to.

However scared of her I am.

Because if I don't, I will die.

And there will be no one here to save me.

GOVERNMENT FEAR

Jennifer Grey, the Minister for Men's Safety, has been speaking to men of their experiences of feeling unsafe in public, and what it is like for them to go out when it's dark, knowing a woman carrying the rapidly spreading STI may lurk just around the corner.

Joseph King, despite having six years of self-defence lessons, feels helpless against a potential attack. He says, "I am always aware that any woman I pass might hurt me."

Fuller Crap states that he always plans to meet his girlfriend at the mid-point of his journey home—that was until he found out his girlfriend was actively seeking to catch the STI from her friends.

"I trusted her," he said. "Then, all along, she was having all these deviant thoughts. One day, I went on her computer and found a pornography website still open. She had searched terms such as 'male on male penis explosion' and 'women with STI gang-bang male.' I was horrified."

We contacted the women's charity, *Not This Woman*, who stated that, "Men need to understand that this isn't a gender thing—it's a deviant thing. Not all women are trying to catch this STI and blow up men's penises—and it is ridiculous to think that."

Meanwhile, Tauks Bullocks, who runs a men's refuge centre in Essex, has found a 250% increase in numbers of men seeking help in the past two weeks.

"Their fears are not unfounded," he says. "Many men live in fear of leaving their wives or girlfriends, and they need our help in doing so. Often, it takes time to convince someone that they have the strength to go, and that is when our refuge is helpful."

Jennifer Grey reminds men they should behave responsibly, such as following the previously released guidelines on how to have a safe night out.

CHAPTER
TWENTY

I WATCH HER GET READY FOR BED.

I imagine it's something a boyfriend or husband wouldn't usually bother watching—but I've never had a relationship before. I've never seen this. And I find it mesmerising how she de-beautifies herself; she wipes her makeup off, changes from a stunning dress to baggy pyjamas, rubs the hairspray out of her hair with dry shampoo—yet she looks far more endearing to me now than she did in the club. Before, she dressed to be the image of perfection—now she is perfection.

It's a shame, really.

That I'm going to have to leave.

I don't want to. Really, I don't. I love her. I've never had this before. The things we do together are things I imagine I could never do with anyone else.

But she scares me.

Right now, it's hard to remind myself how much she scares me. She sees me watching her in the bathroom mirror from my position on the bed, and she smiles at me, her eyes wrinkle, and I feel safe. Everything about her is as I would wish it to be. She redeems herself with a simple curve of her mouth.

I decide not to leave, but just for a minute. I entertain the notion that it's my fault. Which it probably is. I bring the bad side out of her, and this is the real side, and I just need to feed the 'good' side of her better.

I love her. So much. Not just in words, but in my body—I try walking out of the door right now, and my muscles resist the impulse. I will have to force my limbs to betray her, such is the strength of my affection.

But I'll die.

Hey, maybe it's worth it.

Maybe being with her is worth the risk of what she might do.

She catches my eyes again as she wipes a small sponge across her lips, removing any excess lipstick. She winks at me. It's sexy and mischievous.

And I bow my head, sad about the thoughts I've been having.

"What is it?" she asks.

I realise she's still watching me. "Nothing."

She washes her hands, switches the bathroom light off, and sits next to me on the bed.

"Yes, there is. There's something."

I look at her, resting her body weight on her elbow, leaning toward me. How could that face ever hurt anyone?

"I'm fine," I tell her. "Honestly."

"Do you know what fine stands for?"

"What?"

"Freak out, insecure, neurotic and emotional."

I can't help but laugh, but it doesn't last long. I don't feel much like laughing.

"And which one of those am I?" I ask.

"Not sure. Perhaps all the above. Do you know what it also stands for?"

"There's another acronym?"

"It stands for Feelings Inside Not Expressed. Why don't

you tell me what you are feeling inside that you are not expressing?"

I look down at my hands. They play with the string of my pyjama trousers, twiddling it between my fingers and curling it around my thumb.

Why can't she always be like this?

It's so difficult to see her as the person who would risk my life for a quick fuck. Especially when she's like this. When she's trying to be so understanding and accommodating.

Who even is the real Pandora?

"I didn't like that earlier," I tell her.

"I could tell."

I look quizzically at her. I wasn't expecting her to say that, and now she has, I'm not sure why an apology isn't coming.

"You could have killed me."

She shrugs. "I genuinely thought I could control it. Perhaps I was wrong."

"Pandora, I don't think you realise–"

"That you're not like other guys, yeah, I know."

"No! That if we had started having sex, even just a few seconds earlier, then I would be dead right now."

"I think you're being dramatic."

"Dramatic?"

"Yes. We didn't actually have sex. There's no need to be so hysterical."

She makes me question myself. She's so confident and convincing, I wonder if I must be the one in the wrong. Am I overreacting? Am I getting cross about something that's not that big of a deal?

I'm not sure. I feel so confused, and I don't know why.

Am I the problem? Am I irrational? Am I making a big deal out of situations that aren't a big deal?

I wonder how much I know about this woman, and what she's capable of. She says she loves me, and I don't doubt she believes it; but what is love to her? Is it about nurture and growth—or is it about ownership? About possession? About property?

Is love simply a way to exert control over things she doesn't wish to lose?

"How about we get some sleep?" she says. "Maybe you'll feel differently in the morning."

I nod. Maybe I will. Who knows?

She turns away from me, lies down, turns out the light, and pulls my arm around her, forcing me to lie down with her. Her back and buttocks press against my front.

I lay with my eyes open. Her hair smells like coconut, with a faint hint of the smoke machine from the club. She twitches now and then.

I wait for her to fall asleep.

I wait for the gentle snores that signal her slumber, and I slowly take my arm from around her.

And I wait longer.

Just to be careful.

Just to be sure that she will not wake up when I sneak out of that door.

SHE KNOWS

She knows.

She's not an idiot.

He's scared of *her*. *She* can tell by *his* demeanour. *He* is withdrawn—trying to be friendly in the way you would toward a tiger you were trying to tame.

She finds it funny, really. *He* is supposed to love *her*, and instead *he* doubts *her*.

And *she* won't let *him* leave.

Of course *she* won't.

Do you think *she's* a fool?

He's making *his* plans and *his* schemes and *his* plots, and *he* thinks *he* can get to that door without *her* noticing, and *she* is simply waiting, breathing deeply, making *him* think *she's* asleep as *she* orchestrates *his* downfall.

If *he* wants to fuck up the entire foundations of a relationship *she* has worked hard building, then it is up to *him* to face the inevitable consequences.

She leaves the car keys on the table beside the door. *She* makes it easy for *him*. Once *he* finds the opportunity, *he'll* take *his* arm from around *her*, grab those keys, and leave, never to look back.

161

Then *she'll* open *her* eyes.

And *she'll* take *her* time.

No need to rush.

He won't get very far.

She will not be asleep.

She will not be that stupid.

But *he* will.

It happens.

He takes *his* arm. Rolls over. Waits for *her* to stir.

She doesn't stir.

She continues breathing deeply. *She* keeps *her* body still. Even murmurs a little. *She* doesn't know if *she* usually murmurs in *her* sleep, but *he* does, so *she* tries it as well.

He turns *his* legs around. Places *his* feet on the carpet.

At the moment, *he's* safe.

If *she* was to sit up and ask *him* what *he's* doing now, *he* could say *he's* going to the toilet. No suspicion. *She'd* settle back down, and *he'd* return to bed and try again another day.

But *she* doesn't ask *him*—*she* just listens. *She* plays out *his* steps in *her* mind as *she* imagines them happening. Tentative movements, eyes on *her*, constantly checking.

He stands. *He* pauses again.

Oh, *he* is being so very careful.

He takes a step. The bathroom is on *her* side of the bed. The door is on *his*. The closer *he* gets to leaving, the poorer the bathroom excuse becomes.

He could always claim *he* was going out for air. Perhaps *he* can't sleep. Perhaps *he's* struggling to breathe. Perhaps *he's* hot, and *he* wants the breeze of the cool night to soothe *his* perspiring skin.

She still doesn't move. Still listens.

He takes another step. And another. Quiet. Deliberate. Cautious.

The car keys scrape along the wood as *he* lifts them from

the table. *He* remains stationary again. *She* pictures *his* face, staring at *her*, panicked, terrified that *she* will wake up.

She both hates and loves that *he's* scared of *her*. *She* hates that someone *she* loves lives in fear, but is aroused by the power it gives *her*.

The door handle turns.

She could sit up now. *He* could say *he'd* forgotten something in the car. Some gum, perhaps, or water. They keep food in the boot, after all. That could be *his* excuse.

She stays silent. Eyelids closed. Waiting for the right moment.

He picks up *his* shoes. Takes them outside.

The door closes behind *him.*

She opens her eyes.

No need to hurry, *he's* not going anywhere.

She turns over and sees the empty space on the other side of the bed, as if *she* needs confirmation that it's real. *She* laughs. It's funny, isn't it? That *he's* so silly.

She sits up. Stretches *her* arms. *She's* a little cold, so *she* puts on a hoodie. It's one of *his* that *he* left behind. *He* hasn't bothered with any of *his* stuff. *He* didn't have time, and *he* couldn't pack a bag without raising suspicion.

But *he* couldn't even look at *her* without raising suspicion, either. *She* saw deception in every jilted movement. There was nothing safe or subtle about *his* plans—everything was so obvious.

He has no experience of relationships, so *he* has no experience of deception — the key ingredient for any successful romantic endeavour.

And *he* thinks *he* could leave *her*?

He thinks that *she'd* let him?

He thinks *she'd* even give *him* a choice?

She stands. Twitches the curtains. *He's* stepped out of the room, which leads directly into the car park, and is putting *his* shoes on.

She'll wait a bit longer.
Let *him* panic.
And then *she'll* pounce.
Oh, how *she* will pounce.

LAMENTATIONS

CHAPTER
TWENTY-ONE

I CLOSE THE DOOR, STEP INTO THE CAR PARK, AND WAIT.

Listening.

For movement, perhaps. Watching for a flicker of light. Footsteps from inside the room.

There is nothing.

I've made it. She doesn't know.

But I must hurry.

I put my shoes on. Tie my laces. Mess them up. Retie them. Stay calm, Eric, for Christ's sake. You're almost there. Just stay calm.

When my laces are tied, I march to the car and click the lock on the keys.

The car doesn't open. My body seizes. Why isn't it opening?

I press the button again. Still nothing.

It still has an actual key I can use in the lock if the button's not working. So I stick it in. Twist it. The car unlocks. I breathe again.

That was too close.

I sit in the driver's seat. I've taken about twenty lessons, and they were all a year ago, but I'm pretty sure I can remember how to at least start it. I'll be able to get myself a few miles, then I can figure out my next move. I just need to get away.

I glance in the rear-view mirror.

The room is still. Unperturbed. I wonder if she's noticed I'm not next to her. If so, she probably thinks I'm just getting some food from the boot. Hopefully, anyway.

My gaze lingers longer than I'd like it to. I hate leaving her. I want to go back. I urge myself to go back.

I love her.

She can change.

It's all my fault.

These thoughts keep crossing my mind, becoming more pertinent than I care for them to be. I must keep reminding myself: she almost killed me. I said no, and she carried on, and I could have died.

Who's to say she won't do it again?

Stop deliberating, Eric.

You need to hurry.

If she notices I'm not there, then I don't know what she'd do. I'd be in danger. I need to be quick.

I put the key into the ignition.

There is a movement in the rear-view mirror. The door opens. She steps outside.

My entire body tenses. I wait in horror for what happens next.

But she is in no rush.

She hovers by the door, so casually, like it's Sunday morning and she's waiting for the newspaper delivery. She even has a cup of tea in her hands. Has she been up long enough to make a cup of tea? Why didn't she come straight out when she woke up?

The whole situation unsettles me.

I just need to get away. Quickly. She can't get me from the doorway of the hotel room.

I turn the ignition.

Nothing happens.

At first, it doesn't quite make sense. It's strange. Odd, even.

When I turn it again, and not even the lights on the dash-board come to life, it makes sense why she's not chasing after me—*she knows.*

Now she walks toward me. Sauntering across the car park. She wears my hoodie over her pyjamas. She is barefoot, but the uneven cement of the car park doesn't bother her.

I click the lock on the key. The car doesn't lock. Dammit.

I shove the lock down in the door next to me. I leap across the passenger side and shove that lock down too.

She's almost at the car.

She's walking really slowly, but she's almost here.

I reach across the backseats and lock those doors too.

I don't know where I'm going to go now.

I'm trapped.

Damn.

She pauses by the driver's window. Watches me. Sips her tea. Sighs.

"Oh, Eric," she says, like I've been called into the princi-pal's office for something silly, like cheating on an end-of-term maths test; I'm in trouble, and it's because of my own stupid mistake.

I try the ignition again. Maybe it will work.

It doesn't.

I turn it again. And again. And again, and again, and again.

She rattles her knuckles against the window, and it makes me jump.

"I disconnected the battery," she tells me, then takes a last sip of her tea.

She places her mug down on the kerb.

"Why don't you open the door?" she says.

I shake my head. Not a chance. Nope, not a chance. I will stay here and starve if I have to. I will not go back in there and face what she'll do to me.

"If you just open the door and come back inside voluntarily, then I will make this a lot nicer for you."

I shake my head as vehemently as I can.

I'm also crying.

Stop crying. It's making you look weak. You need to be strong; you need to stand up to her.

But I don't look strong. I look like a wreck.

She shakes her head, a gesture of pity.

"Fine."

She walks away from me.

For a moment, I am relieved.

Then she approaches a fence that seals off some work that's being done at the edge of the car park. There are mounds of dirt and diggers, all waiting for the workmen to arrive in the morning.

She jumps onto the fence, digs her fingers between the criss-crossed wires, and climbs up. It doesn't take long for her to reach the top and climb over. She lands on her feet and looks back and forth.

She is distracted by something to her right. I'm not sure what.

I try the ignition again. I don't know why; she's disconnected the battery. Maybe I should get out and reconnect it?

But I wouldn't have a clue what I was doing.

Maybe I should unlock the door and make a run for it?

She could probably catch me. But I have a head start now. Maybe I could–

She reappears. She has something in her hand. It's silver and glistens in the moonlight. She climbs over the fence, and any thought I had of unlocking this car door and running disappears.

I should have been quicker.

I should have taken my chance.

But, somehow, it feels safer in this car. I can lock the doors and hope that, when morning comes, someone will arrive and help me.

Then again, would anyone even believe me? If she battered her eyelashes and flashed them a smile, she could make a stranger think anything.

It doesn't matter. I must wait a few hours, that's all. Morning will come, and someone will be here.

Except, that's no longer the case.

Because she is approaching me, and I see what is in her hand.

It's a wrench.

A large metal wrench.

One that could easily smash through a car window.

CHAPTER
TWENTY-TWO

SHE SMASHES THE WINDOW, REACHES INSIDE, GRABS MY THROAT and starts to pull me out. I put my hands up and I say, "Okay, okay, I'll come out!"

She stands back. Waits. Taps the wrench against her thigh. She makes sure I look at it. One strike against my skull and I'm on the floor.

I've never been as scared of a person as I am of her right now.

I open the door. She grabs my collar, and she drags me out and I land on the ground and she stands over me and tells me to get up.

I do so, with my hands in the air, held aloft by weak arms and a weak mind.

She lets me stand there. Watches me. Laughs. I don't blame her. I'm pathetic.

Then her demeanour changes. She steps closer. I flinch. She runs her hand down my cheek and smiles that smile I've seen so many times before. The one that makes my knees shake. And I see the real Pandora; the one that lies beneath.

"Why would you try to run away from me?" she says. "Don't you know how much I love you?"

I feel ashamed. And I feel confused. I feel sad and happy and angry and calm and panicked and reassured.

I feel everything and nothing. I am manically numb.

She is the love of my life. She is the source of all my pain.

She leans her forehead against mine. I smell her sweat. She still holds the wrench in her spare hand. I don't watch it. I watch her. Relishing being close, and her being the true Pandora—finally, she is here.

"Shall we go back inside?" she asks. "And we can talk about this in the morning?"

I sniff. Am I crying? I think so, but I don't know why. It's relief or fear. Maybe both.

"Come on, why don't we–"

She stops. Something distracts her. She lifts her head to the side and squints, like she's trying hard to hear something.

I don't hear it at first; then I do. Faint sirens. In the distance.

Those sirens could be for anything, but it feels like they aren't just for anything.

She glares at something over my shoulder so intently I can't help but look to see what it is. It's the receptionist, looking out of the window at us, with a phone by his ear.

"You prick," she growls.

The sirens get louder. There's so many of them. This isn't just a single car coming for us; it's a whole convoy.

"Get back inside," she tells me.

I consider resisting, but I don't, and her fingers grip my forearm with such force that it hurts. I glance over my shoulder as she drags me back to the hotel room. The sirens become so loud it is all I can focus on. Curtains twitch in other rooms; the voyeurs getting ready to spy on the big showdown.

She shoves me inside and locks the door. She turns all lights off, opens the curtains just a smidge, and peers out.

From over her shoulder, I can make out glimpses of police

cars. There are quite a few of them. They form a semi-circle. Some of them have guns. Do they really fear us so much that they sent a firearms unit?

Then again, how many deaths are we responsible for? It would make sense that they would chase us with urgency and take no precautions.

She notices me peering over her shoulder.

"Get on the bed," she tells me.

I go to object, then she raises the wrench in the air.

I lay on the bed.

She watches the furore outside, and I watch her for a reaction, wishing I could see what's going on. Her focus is so emotionless; so business-like. There's a problem, and she's going to solve it.

"This is the police!" a voice shouts. "Let Eric go and come out!"

Let me go?

Why do they want her to let me go?

It dawns on me: they think I'm a victim. That I'm being held hostage. That Pandora is the villain, and I've had no choice in the matter.

Is that why they aren't entering—because they are trying to keep me safe?

Pandora looks to her feet and sighs. Bites her lip. Concentrates. There are so many thoughts going through her mind, I can see her computing them, mulling over her options. Surrender. Fight. Run. Whatever it is, she entertains every possibility.

And I cannot decide whether I want them to catch her.

I made my way to the car, and I was going to escape—but how far would I have gone before I turned back?

I want to be free of the dark side of this woman. I want to go where I want, when I want to. But I also do not want them to take her away from me.

My yearning for her is beyond primitive. It is emotional; it is carnal; it is deep and longing. My love grows every time I look at her, and to see the pain in her face, even in the brief flickers between various contemplations, hurts me more than I could ever let on.

Her eyes focus on me. They hover there. As if she is now considering how I can be factored into her plan.

"Do you trust me?" she asks.

"What?"

"I said, do you trust me?"

It's not a simple question. It should be, but it's not.

"Yes," I finally say.

She strides toward me, stopping at the end of the bed and covering me in her shadow. "How much do you trust me?"

"With my life."

She nods. This is what she wants to hear.

She marches to the bag that she stuffed in the corner when we first arrived. She goes through it, takes out some duct tape, and walks back toward me.

"What are you doing?" I ask, recoiling away from her.

She kneels on the end of the bed. "I thought you said you trust me with your life?"

I pause. I did say that. I did say that I trust her with my life.

"Or were you lying?"

I watch her. I can't tell if she's hurt or if she's manipulating me. I've never had a relationship before; I don't know if this constant state of confusion is how it's meant to be.

"I wasn't lying," I tell her.

"Then you need to do what I say."

"But–"

"I don't have time to explain, Eric."

I consider this, then nod.

"Lift your arms up and put your wrists together," she instructs.

I hesitate, then lift my hands up and put my wrists together.

She places the duct tape against my skin, and it's sticky and hard, and she wraps it around my wrists, not just once but again and again, then interweaves it around my individual wrists, then around both my wrists again. Once she is done, and she's ripped away the end of the masking tape, my hands are bound so tightly, and with such a large quantity of tape, that there is not a chance I could escape from my bindings.

She places the tape on the bedside table, then watches me. She is deep in thought.

"What are you thinking?" I ask.

She doesn't reply. She strides back to the bag and returns to my side with scissors. At first, I think she is about to release my hands, but instead, she puts the blades of the scissors at the bottom of my t-shirt and drags them upwards, cutting my top in half until she exposes my chest.

"Pandora?"

She runs the blades down the sleeves until she can pull the fabric away.

"Pandora, what is this?"

Then she undoes my belt, pulls my trousers down, then my underwear.

She leaves my socks on, though, and it makes me feel even more humiliated; nothing looks weirder than a man wearing nothing but socks.

"Pandora, why am I naked? I don't understand?"

"Shut up, Eric, I'm trying to think."

"Pandora," comes the voice from outside. "We know you have Eric in there with you. Let him go, and step outside, and we promise you will not get hurt."

They don't seem to realise that the longer they leave me in here with her, the more perilous my position becomes.

"Pandora, I don't understand why I–"

"I said shut up."

She peers between the crack in the curtains again. Thinks. Then collects the masking tape and straddles my chest.

"Pandora? I–"

She sticks the masking tape across my lips. The prickles of hair that makes up a moustache I can barely grow hurts as she applies the sticky side of the tape. She wraps the tape around the back of my head, then back around my mouth.

It's tight and pressing against the base of my skull. I try objecting, but it's muffled, and she wraps the tape around my mouth again, so tight that even if I were to try and scream, I would struggle to move my mouth, or even emit a sound.

Now I lie here, like an animal being brought to slaughter, and stare at her, waiting to hear this plan she has.

She peers out of the window again.

"I'm going to do something now," she says. "And if you love me, you will understand why."

She holds my gaze, and her stare feels lovingly demented; affectionately sadistic; and I don't think letting her tie my hands was a good idea.

"Great love requires great sacrifice, Eric. I hope you realise that."

With another glance out of the window, she returns to the end of the bed and strips. Her top first, then her trousers. Even the perfect curves of her body feel ominous. Everything about her screams *sex*, and my dick grows hard against my better judgement, and I wish I was back home with Mother and Father, laughing with my sister, going to church group, doing work for university.

I should never have left.

She unclips her bra and lets it drop to the floor. Steps out of her underwear. She removes her socks. She climbs over the edge of the bed and grabs me.

I can't ask her what she's doing, so I hope she reads the question in my eyes.

She does.

And she tells me.

"I'm going to fuck you," she states, matter of fact, like she's saying *I'm about to eat this cheeseburger* or *this waffle is delicious.*

I will myself not to get harder. She can't do anything if I'm soft and limp.

But my body betrays me. So unused to a woman's touch, the more she rubs it, the stiffer it gets.

And I know, in this moment, with absolute certainty, that I am about to die for the woman I love—and that she has not given me a choice.

To her, I'm just a man.

To her, I'm worthless.

She has the power. I must honour and obey. If someone needs to be sacrificed, it must be me.

She places my penis inside of her, and I feel the warmth of sex for the very first time.

SHE FUCKS HIM

She fucks *him*.

She fucks *him* like *she* was fucked as a child—by a man who called himself Uncle despite being no relation whatsoever.

He was a family friend. Someone *her* father trusted.

Someone *her* father still trusts.

They still share a beer at Christmas and a sofa during the World Cup and a phone call of support during a grievance. *Her* father trusts him, and *she* has never told him why he shouldn't. *She's* not sure why *she's* never admitted the truth. Perhaps *she* wouldn't know what *she* would do if he didn't believe *her*.

She still sees Uncle in photographs with *her* parents, but Uncle's not interested in *her* anymore.

There is no power to be had over an adult. A child is yet to be damaged. A young girl is a plank of wood, resistant to the trauma, and now *she's* paper, easily ripped, and if Uncle grabbed *her, she* would just crumple or blow away on the wind.

Sometimes, *she* considers the audacity of Uncle remaining in her parents' lives. He does not fear the repercussions of any confession *she* could make as an adult. He does not avoid *her* father to avoid being accused. He stays around, as if to show that he is invincible.

If *she* said anything now, there would be no reason for anyone to believe *her*.

There is no evidence to corroborate *her* story.

Her teacher said *she* was becoming withdrawn. Not as spritely as *she* used to be. They spoke about it at parent's evening. But that was it. There were no further questions; *she* was just an introverted child, and the bruising was too deep below *her* clothes for them to see.

There were videos.

Uncle took videos.

Sometimes, *she* wonders where those videos are. How much they go for. If they are still circulating. If paedophiles still masturbate to *her* childish body.

So *she* fucks *him*. Eric. Fucks him like *he* wants; like *he's* never had.

He doesn't realise how good *he* has it; *she'd* kill to lose her virginity at twenty-six, rather than lose it at nine.

She tries to focus. To concentrate. *She* wills herself to enjoy it. But it's hard to fuck any man without returning to an age *she* never grew past. *She* will forever be a child, waiting for adolescence.

They say abusers have often been abused themselves.

But *she's* not an abuser. *She's* a fucker. A revenge-artist. *She* is a woman for those few minutes where *she* needs to be a woman; just as *she* was a woman for those long hours when *she* was a girl.

Uncle.

Why did *she* have to call him Uncle?

Why did Dad never see it?

She hates Uncle. *She* hates Dad. *She* hates them all.

They all do this.

They say they don't, but they do.

That honourable man; that doctor or politician or inspirational speaker; delve deep enough into their past, and you'll find it. An indiscretion. A reason they deserve it.

She fucks *him*.

Oh boy, does *she* fuck *him*.

It's *his* first and last, and *she* wishes to give *him* a show.

She does all the things Uncle taught *her*.

Those are the things men always like.

The rotation of *her* hips, the staring into their eyes, the tongue hanging loosely out of *her* mouth, the pleading for their cum, the grunts on each thrust, the begs for more, the hands on their chest, the pushing it deeper inside of her, the touching herself, the constant verbal encouragement that it's the biggest and best cock *she's* ever had in *her* tight little cunt.

It's a poor imitation of pornography, but it's what they want, isn't it?

Uncle used to say how tight it was, and *she's* not met a man who hasn't craved the same.

She fucks *him*.

Over and over.

It lasts longer than normal, because *she* teases *him*, and keeps *him* going for longer. Why not? If this is the only sex *he* will ever know, *she* may as well make it worth it.

It was good while it lasted, after all. *He* was a man who loved *her* but never wanted to fuck *her*. *She* never had to put on an act for *him*. Until now.

She gives *him* a performance Uncle would have been proud of. He was always such an excellent teacher. *She* loved making him proud. Perhaps that's the toughest part—admitting that *she* liked the attention. That's when the guilt sets in, and *she* stops thinking about it, and concentrates on the dick inside of *her*.

It would never be as big as Uncle's.

At least, it will never feel as big.

She fucks *him*.

She grinds and grinds and screams and screams and the police shout and *she* wants to tell them not to worry, it's almost over, *he's* just about there.

He isn't like the rest of them.

She cackles.

Looks down at the face of the man who says *he* loves *her*, vulnerable and perplexed.

He is *exactly* the same as the rest of them.

CHAPTER
TWENTY-THREE

I DON'T EVEN MOVE.

I thought I'd struggle or fight or scream. But I don't. My thoughts are manic, but my body is lethargic. Relaxed, even. Like I'm unable to move even if I wish to. My body is rigid. My hands are numb.

It's as if I'm playing dead. Like you're supposed to when you get attacked by a bear. I lay limply to show there is nothing there. She is grinding back and forth over something empty.

Then my body comes alive. It responds to the pleasure. I may not have willed this to happen, and I may have fought it if my body allowed it, but I can't help what happens next.

My dick gets harder. My heart rate increases. I feel what every other man is motivated by. It's sickeningly glorious. It's a feeling of warm moisture tight around my penis. It makes masturbation feel pointless. Like every time I've sat there with my boxers around my ankles in front of my computer, I've been convincing myself it was a good enough substitute for the real thing—but it's not. It never could be. Nothing has ever felt like this.

Her perky nipples get hard. I feel like I'm in an erotic

novel, forced to be submissive, not given a choice and unclear whether this is a good or a bad thing.

She looks me in the eyes.

I'm not sure what I see.

It looks like pleasure; like ecstasy. Like she is experiencing pure, unadulterated brilliance. Like she's waited for this for so long.

But it also looks like arrogance. Like a triumphant victory. Like she knows what I don't know; like she's been in control since the beginning, and I have been subservient to her every whim.

She moves quicker.

The police keep shouting. I don't hear what they say, but I know it's pointless. But they'll wait. We are the ones who will run out of food. We are the ones who cannot change shifts. They will wait as long as it takes.

But it won't take long.

She's speeding up, and I can feel my body responding. I will myself not to. If I don't climax, then I don't die. Is that how it works? I'm not sure. Maybe she's already given it to me, and now it's just a matter of time.

That time is arriving.

My breathing quickens pace. My body prepares. The point of no return comes and goes.

And I cum so long and so hard that I can't tell where the ceiling or the floor is anymore. She's screaming too but I'm concentrating on my side of it, and she finishes cumming but I'm still going, it's still sensitive, she's still moving even though I'm finished and my body is jolting and twitching on every subtle thrust.

Then she stops.

Looks down at me.

And smiles that smile.

"Thank you," she says.

It's a strange thing to say.

For what, I attempt to muffle through the gag.

"You're about to save me."

She stands. She leaves a sticky splodge on the bedsheet. She dresses.

I lie here, waiting for it to happen.

But she doesn't wait. As soon as she has a dress on, she is dragging me to my feet, and she is forcing me to stand on legs that still shake.

She shoves me toward the door. I stumble, and she shoves me again, then she holds the door handle, but doesn't open it. Not yet. She stays close to me, enough that I can feel her breath against my cheeks.

I want to tell her I love her, but the tape restricts my mouth, so I tell her with my eyes; if that's even possible.

"I love you, too," she tells me.

She leans her forehead against mine. Touches our noses. Then kisses me on the forehead, and it feels special; like she's never kissed anyone there before.

I wish I knew more about her. I wish I knew her past. I wish I knew why.

And, as I think about all the little things I don't know, it occurs to me that she's never revealed what she was studying at university. In fact, I don't think anyone else in the Christian society recognised her, and she didn't have a student ID lanyard around her neck and I wonder—was she even a student?

And if she wasn't, why was she there?

The realisation arrives, and I pull away from her kiss, and see her in a way I've never seen her before.

I still can't talk. My lips are bound. But it's as if she sees what I'm thinking, and I don't even need to ask.

"No, I wasn't a student."

My dick throbs.

It's happening.

"I was looking for you specifically."

I want to punch it, but I can't.

I focus on her.

I have to know.

I beseech her with my eyes, as much as I think I am able.

"You want to know why, don't you?"

I nod my head. Ignore the pain. It's swelling, and it's agony.

"Your father," she tells me, rubbing a hand down my cheek—no longer affectionate, but patronising. "I knew him, once…"

It hurts. So much. Like a million bees swarming around my bellend.

But I focus as much as I can on what she says next.

"You call him Father. I used to call him Uncle."

I frown. I don't understand. But it is too late for answers.

She opens the door and shoves me out. Artificial lights shine on me, and I squint as my dick expands, and the police approach me.

SHE ESCAPES

She escapes.

It's *her* best opportunity.

Police gather around *him*. *He* can't tell them not to. The tape around *his* mouth sees to that.

They are fools. Their attention diverted by the obvious distraction. *Her* plan has worked just as *she* intended it to.

She enters the bathroom. There is a window above the shower. *She* climbs onto the toilet and uses the open frame to pull *herself* up. *She* slithers out and lands on the pavement.

Just around the alleyway, they swarm toward *Eric*.

Poor, innocent little *Eric*.

They gather around *him* with no thought of what is about to happen.

She waits.

Listens to the sympathetic men being sympathetic toward the *poor man* who's been so badly injured.

… oh, Eric, how sad it is that you were abused in such a way, how disgusting, what a horrible woman, see women do hurt men too, if this was the other way around we'd be in uproar, this is absolutely representative of the issue as a whole, and we are in no way

sympathetic toward you because you are a white male like us, oh please, where is the ambulance, let's see to your wound...

Their sympathy will be their downfall.

They swarm around *him* to help, unaware of what will happen.

Their desperation to help brings them closer to *him*.

... oh, you poor man, you upstanding citizen, you middle-class academic, you mild-mannered male, everything about you reeks of good character, oh how could a woman do this to you, oh please contact all the charities, he's naked too, she took away his pride, oh his male ego oh how much it will hurt, he is so virtuous, how could such an evil woman hurt such a man like this, men are victims too oh yes they are oh how they are...

She peers around the corner of the alleyway. Watches them being so caring. Watches them dote upon the poor, defence-less *Eric*.

They are honourable police officers, all male, all doing what they can to make a difference.

But *she* sees them for what they are. And, in the worst possible way, *she'd* be willing to fuck every one of them.

The young man who's just qualified as an officer = the dickhead who groped a woman's arse in the nightclub and told her he hadn't done anything.

The family man who's looking to advance his career by being promoted to sergeant = the one who tells his wife she's being emotional and to stop making everything his fault.

The older inspector teaching the young men how to make a difference in such a stressful job = the man with old-fash-ioned views that society deemed acceptable in his day and therefore makes him sceptical whenever a weak-willed hysterical woman comes to him with accusations against a man in power. That man did charity work, they will need to make sure they have hell of a lot of evidence if they are to go against him, and she was very flirtatious, so she must have been asking for it!

Hey, Mr Older Inspector Guy, do you know what is really impossible to get hold of when trying to prove lack of consent? EVIDENCE.

... oh Eric how could she do this to you you're such an honourable young man with so much promise the trauma will be immense how could she ruin a young man's life how could she all these accusations and these things she's done she's scarred you for life how could she what a monster what an absolute monster all women are monsters all women manipulate men all women are evil oh how you are such a victim...

His dick expands.

She is growing tired of this outpouring of empathy toward *him*.

Once the explosion occurs, they will be even more distracted, and *she* will run.

And *she* will escape.

And *she* will get to fuck again.

CHAPTER
TWENTY-FOUR

I BEG THEM NOT TO COME CLOSER, BUT EVERY WORD I SAY IS muffled. I barely make a sound—just an attempt at sound constricted by tape wrapped so tightly around my head that I struggle to breathe.

They run toward me. Most of them. They gather around me, trying to help, trying to find scissors to cut the tape off, putting a jacket around me to preserve my dignity. They are so eager to assist me that they don't see my dick expanding, growing, the bellend shining orange.

I turn to run, hoping I can save them by putting distance between us, but I fall over, landing on my penis, covering the potential bomb ticking down, tick tock tick tock tick tock...

"Son, come with us."

"It's going to be okay."

"Come on, let's get you untied."

Let me go let me go let me go!

I want to shout it at them, scream it at them, roar at them: *Can't you see my dick? I'm naked, can't you see what it's doing?*

I try to get to my knees but the pain is immense, it's throbbing and pulsating and I'm struggling to concentrate on anything else. Tears stream down my cheeks, my eyes widen,

I stare at the group of officers around me, begging them to read my eyes.

By the time the dick has grown so noticeably large, they can't get away. Some of them try. They run, but it's too late.

And, just before it happens, I glance across the car park, and I see her just around the side of the alleyway.

She stares at me.

I expect to see love. Gratitude. Something grateful for my sacrifice. I am distracting them so she can escape, after all. Who knows if I'd have agreed to do this should I not have been bound and forced—but that's what I have done, and I have done it for the woman I love.

But there is no doting look on her face. No warmth, no sadness at the loss, no sorrow at what she's had to give up.

There is a cocky, knowing, teeth-bearing grin.

And in the final few seconds of my life—which seem to stretch to accommodate my anguish and fury—I see her for what she is.

She didn't want someone to love; she wanted someone to control.

And I am a sucker for being that person.

I want to raise my middle finger. Shout at her. Bark obscenities, tell her she's a bitch, a whore, a slut, and that I regret the day I danced on the blood of my housemate with her.

I thought we were doing something right, but in truth, we were just doing something.

Then there's a moment when it stops hurting.

And a life of doing nothing wrong crosses my mind. It omits any acts of evil, and I see how great I was for the world.

Then the explosion occurs.

I don't die straight away.

The world's too out of focus for me to see the wayward blood and puss and pieces of my anatomy that scatter across the car park—and it's too out of focus for me to see the police officers who end up covered in the various juices strewn from my vacant crotch.

There's just enough time for me to feel the absence between my legs, and to feel the hole, and the throbbing, and the vulnerability of it, and my body slows down, and my insides drop out, and my brain gives up.

And I am paralysed, laying on the floor, my head on the cement, watching blood trickle toward the drain.

In the distance, Pandora's feet patter away, disguised by the pandemonium I slowly grow deaf to.

The ringing in my ears is loud, and once sound becomes my only remaining sense, it gets even louder, until it overcomes my fading consciousness.

Then I'm just an empty face with wide eyes lying on the tarmac outside of a cheap hotel.

I wasn't so different from the rest of them in the end.

She fucked me and left me for dead.

I guess that means it's all over.

MALACHAI

SHE CONTINUES

She continues without *him*.

He was never vital to the plan, anyway.

In fact, it's easier without *him* watching.

She watches the news. *She* never used to. *She* didn't enjoy watching stories of murdered girls and what women wear to award ceremonies and wives not being good wives.

Now, the news is delightful to watch.

Every day, another man is scared for his life. Every day, another man holds onto his keys when he passes a group of women. Every day, men watch the way they dress so they don't attract unwanted advances that will end up with their penis exploding.

And it is all thanks to *her*.

Men hunt *her*. Women worship *her*.

Whenever police arrive at *her* door, women from an adjacent building or flat block or restaurant or park or street corner flood the exterior of *her* location to allow *her* to escape.

Never in a way that is easily noticeable, of course. It is done in a way that is purely coincidental—and, even if the civilian's actions create too much of an inconvenience for the police, they spend a night in the cells with a smile on their face, grateful that they could help *her*.

She rewrites the books. Rewrites the movies. Rewrites religions. Everything is geared toward *her* now. *She* wears short skirts and low-cut tops, and men look away from *her* as they walk past, desperate not to give any false signals, eager to show they are not interested in *her* advances, compelled to ensure they don't get hurt.

And for those men who don't look away? Those who still have the audacity?

Well, *she* happily has sex with them. What a treat. What a surprise. A woman who wants to fuck them within minutes of meeting? Oh, this hardly ever happens, oh how lucky I must be, how fortunate, my wife will never know, shall we get a hotel room I'll pay for it, oh you are so attractive, I am not at all suspicious that a woman as attractive as you is willing to spontaneously sleep with an overweight middle-aged man like me, it happens all the time in porn, no foreplay even better, four minutes and done, that was great, that was, hey, what's this, what's… splat.

She misses *him* in those moments. The ones where the walls are decorated, and the body lays empty on the bed. It was special, being able to frolic and play together.

But any sadness passes quickly.

She is proud of what *she's* done.

Even so, there is a large part of *her* mission still incomplete. Something on the list remains undone.

Just one thing *she* is yet to do.

Despite all *she's* accomplished, *she* cannot be happy until it's done.

And, on a day that *she* will, in the future, refer to as *Judgement Day, she* approaches a house *she* remembers differently. It was a lot bigger, and the garden didn't have as many flowers, and the tree outside was smaller.

There is a constant feeling of grief around this house.

Anyone who enters or exits does so with solace and melancholy. Like they've just lost someone close to them.

She pulls up behind a BMW and doesn't bother to lock *her* car. Who would dare steal from *her*?

She saunters up the path, *her* hips swaying, each square foot of garden conjuring childhood memories that prompt a delightful pain.

There's the bench where *she* once sat when *she* was supposed to be at school. He said he'd give *her* a lift. He didn't. His child was at school, though *she* never got to meet *his* child. *He* was lucky—*he* was a boy, and boys weren't his thing. Little girls were.

He stood in front of that bench and said they were going to play a game. *She* would be Maid Marian. He would be Robin Hood. He would introduce her to his Merry Men.

Behind the bench, the garden gnome, holding a fishing rod with a grin on his face despite never having caught anything. *She* used to think that gnome came alive and spied on *her*. That, if *she* told anyone, the gnome would get *her*. Did he tell *her* that would happen or was that *her* imagination? *She* isn't sure. But *she* believed it.

Oh, boy, how *she* believed it.

She pauses by the front door. The welcome mat is new. The door's a different colour. Once it was white, now it is black. But the door knocker is the same. It has the face of a gargoyle.

She knocks on the door.

She steps back. There is a small tree in the middle of the garden. A young tree. One that's still growing. A plaque in front of it reads *For our dear son, Eric.*

There is shuffling from behind the door. It opens. A man stands there.

He has less hair. His belly is bigger. His movements are jilted—slower. He doesn't recognise *her*. Perhaps he shouldn't. *She* looks a lot different. *She* has breasts now, for a start. And hips. And confidence. He wasn't used to that.

He's friends with *her* father, but *she* hasn't spoken to *her* father in years, unwilling to form an adult bond with the man who raised her.

Her father doesn't understand why. But this man does.

This man does.

He goes to open his mouth, his double chin wobbling, but he doesn't speak. He wants to ask how he can help *her*, but a vague recollection pricks his memory. The shape of *her* face is familiar. Not *her* body, but the way *she* holds it.

She smiles widely. *Her* eyes don't wrinkle.

"Hello, Uncle," *she* says, and *she* steps past him, into the house of The Devil.

For only when *you* defeat The Devil, can *you* truly say *you* have conquered evil.

People can argue with *her* logic, but *her* followers fiercely defend *her*.

She closes the door and does not leave until it is done.

She doesn't need to see the look on his wife's face. If his wife knows anything about him, she'll understand.

And *she* leaves, looking up at the sun and enjoying the warmth on *her* face. *She* has accomplished all *she* needs to accomplish. The world is a different place now. *She* has created it as *she* wishes it to be.

See, this is not a story about how *she* becomes like the people *she* hates. It is not a story about how *she* abuses men, or how *she* conquers men; it is not even a story about how *she* turns the pain caused by *her* enemies on themselves.

Oh no, my dear friends, this is now a story about how *she* becomes a hero.

This is a story about how *she* becomes a *god*.

JOIN RICK WOOD'S
READER'S GROUP...

And get **Roses Are Red So Is Your Blood** for free!

Join at **www.rickwoodwriter.com/sign-up**

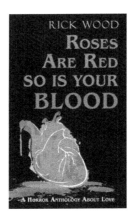

BLOOD
SPLATTER
BOOKS

WOMAN
SCORNED

RICK WOOD

18+

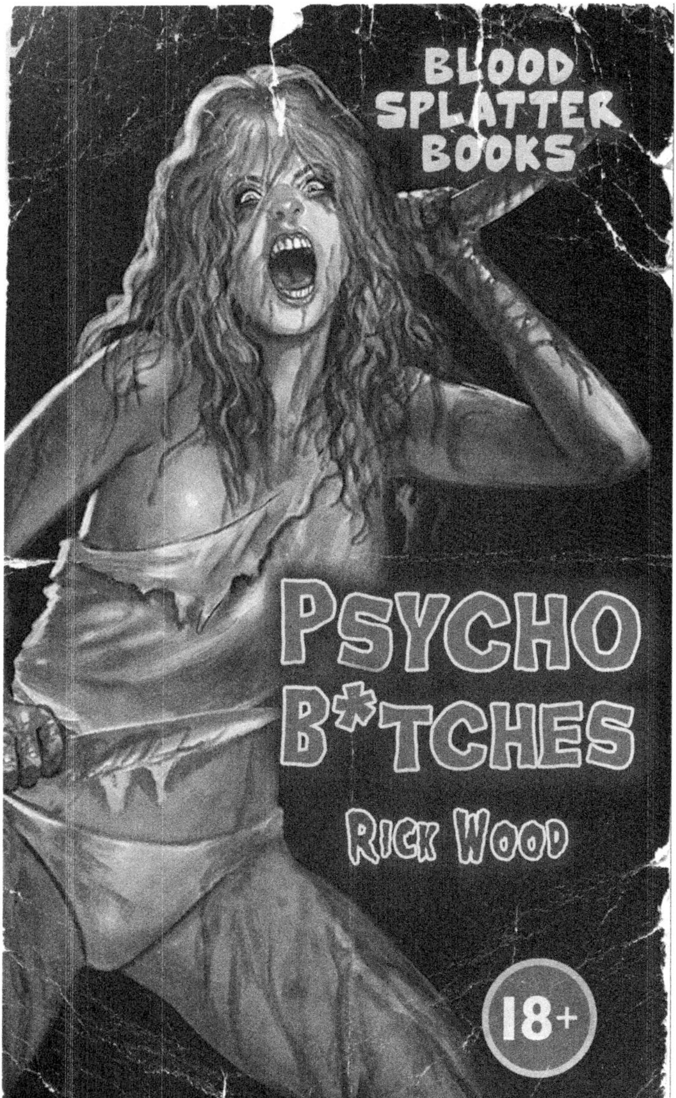
BLOOD SPLATTER BOOKS
PSYCHO B*TCHES
RICK WOOD
18+

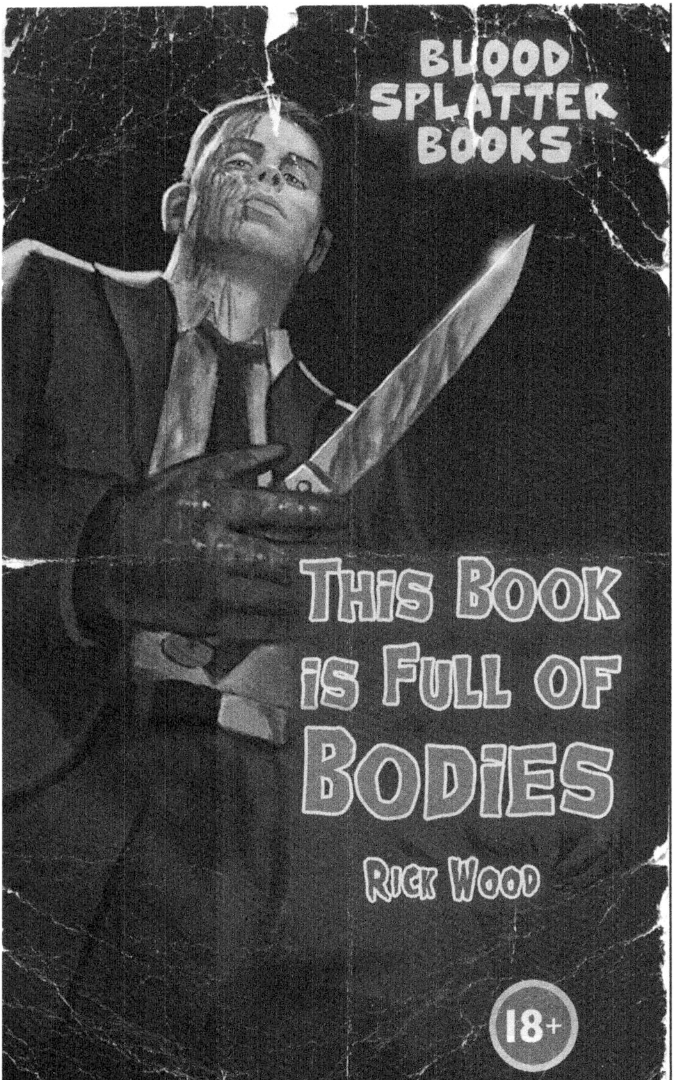
BLOOD SPLATTER BOOKS
THIS BOOK IS FULL OF BODIES
RICK WOOD
18+

BLOOD
SPLATTER
BOOKS

SHUTTER
HOUSE

Rick Wood

18+

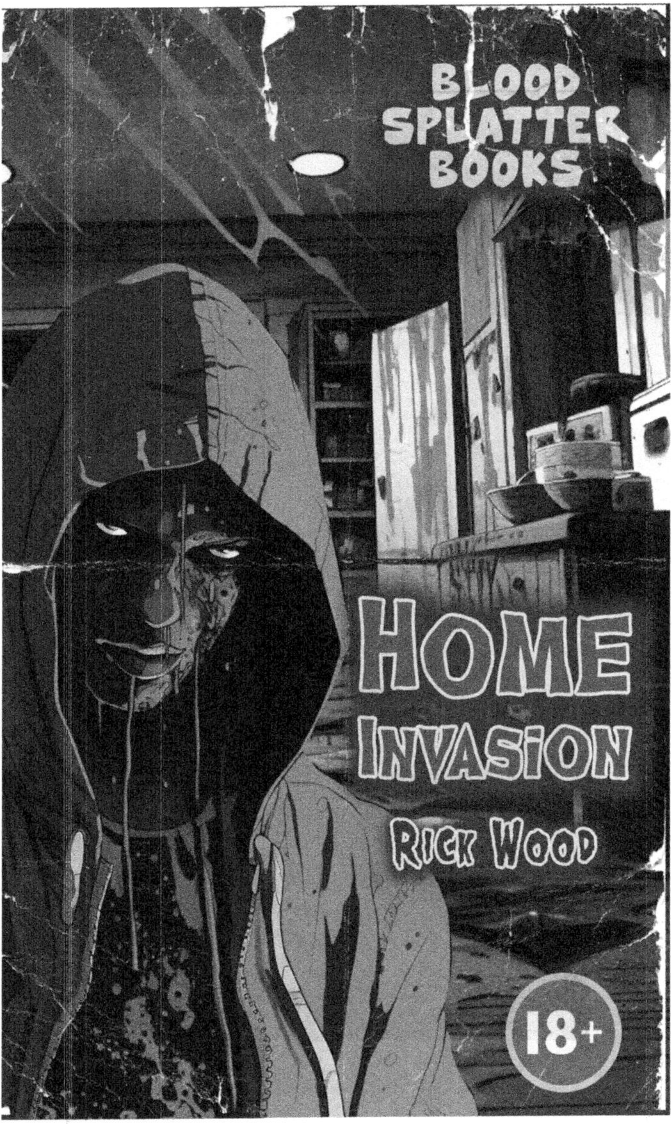
BLOOD
SPLATTER
BOOKS
HOME
INVASION
RICK WOOD
18+

BLOOD
SPLATTER
BOOKS
HAUNTED
HOUSE
RICK WOOD
18+

ALSO BY RICK WOOD...

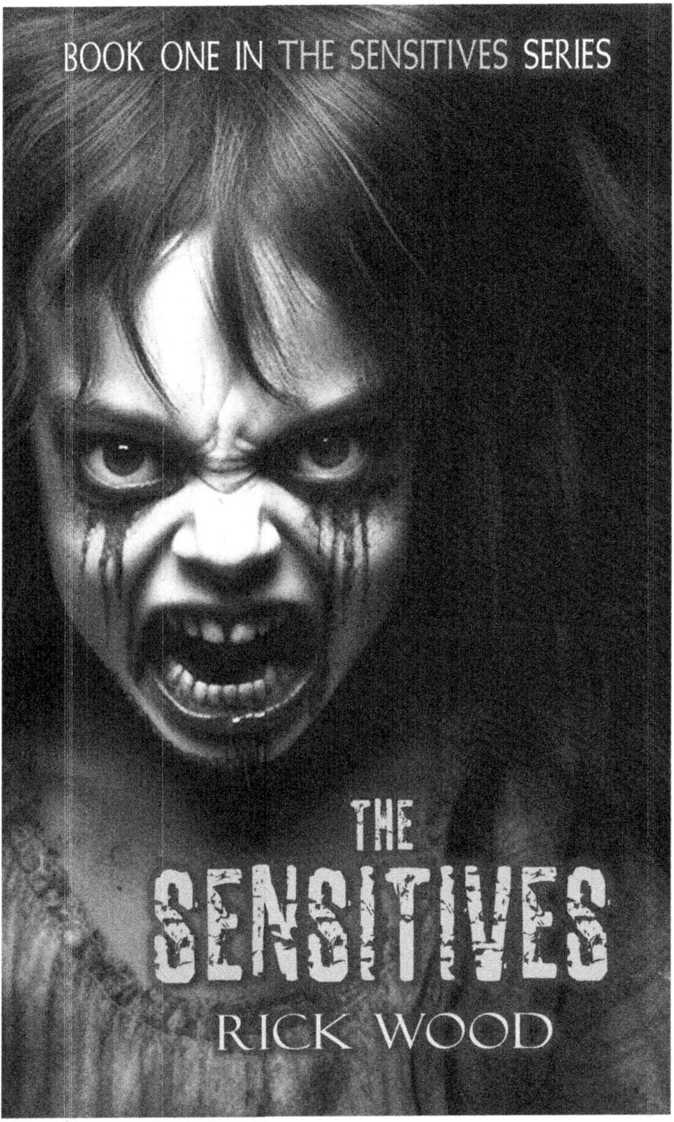
BOOK ONE IN THE SENSITIVES SERIES
THE SENSITIVES
RICK WOOD

THE HAUNTING
OF EVIE MEYERS

RICK WOOD

Printed in Great Britain
by Amazon